Buddhist Animal Wisdom Stories

Buddhist Animal Wisdom Stories

Illustrated
and retold by
Mark W. McGinnis

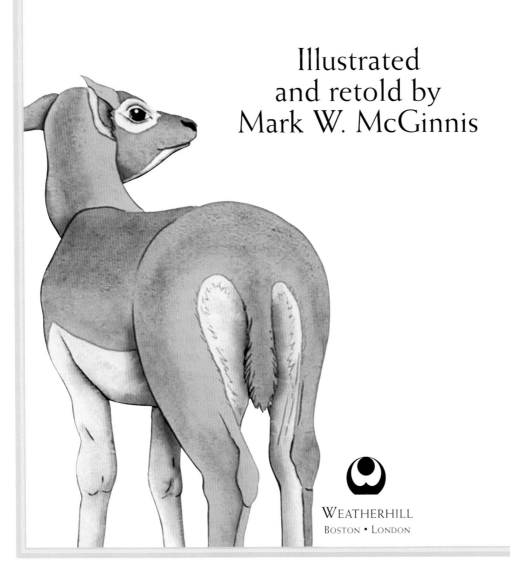

WEATHERHILL
BOSTON • LONDON

Dedicated to my grandson Gabriel Rowan McGinnis

Weatherhill
An imprint of Shambhala Publications, Inc.
Horticultural Hall
300 Massachusetts Avenue
Boston, Massachusetts 02115
www.shambhala.com

10 9 8 7 6 5 4

Printed in China

♾ This edition is printed on acid-free paper that meets the American National
Standards Institute Z39.48 Standard. ♻ Shambhala Publications makes every effort to
print on recycled paper. For more information please visit www.shambhala.com.
Distributed in the United States by Random House, Inc., and in Canada by
Random House of Canada Ltd

Library of Congress Cataloging-in-Publication Data available upon request.

ISBN 978-0-8348-0551-4

Contents

INTRODUCTION

I first became aware of Buddhist animal wisdom stories when I was a graduate student at the university of Illinois, Champaign-Urbana, in the early 1970s. Along with my major in painting, I also pursued a minor in Oriental art history. It was then that I first encountered Buddhism and I was immediately drawn to its gentle, introspective spiritual path. I can recall my professor's lectures on the Indian relief carvings depicting the Jataka tales, the stories of the Buddha's previous reincarnations, some of which were in various animal forms.

That stimulus lay dormant for twenty years until the early 1990s, when I was working on a body of paintings based on Lakota and Dakota animal wisdom stories. As I was working on this series I recalled the Buddhist stories and decided to do a project based on the Jataka tales. I had since become a practicing lay Buddhist and wished to use my talents to express some of the qualities I had discovered in my studies of Buddhism.

The 1990s, however, became filled with other projects dealing with world religions and two series of portraits and interviews with religious elders. When I was finishing the last group of portraits in 1999, I began to research the Jataka tales and prepare my long-delayed series on Buddhist animal wisdom stories. I found that the Jataka was a body of ancient Pali Buddhist scriptures that described five hundred fifty previous lives of the Buddha before his birth as Gautama, the prince of the Shakya clan. When this occurred in the late sixth century B.C.E., he attained complete enlightenment that released him from any future rebirth. This process of the Buddha's evolution through numerous lives is in accord with the widely held Indian belief in karma. In its simplest form, karma is the law of cause and effect, the principal that everything we do in this life shapes our current existence as well as our next. In his five hundred fifty previous lives, the Buddha had existed in a multitude of animal and human forms. In each life, his noble and compassionate deeds moved him higher toward his final greatness and emancipation.

I searched for published translations of animal Jatakas, sometimes finding four or five versions of the same story. To conclude my research, at the end of 1999 I made a three-week trip to India. My intent was to travel the Buddhist pilgrimage path for my personal spiritual growth and to search for more Jataka tales. I also planned to do sketches and photographic research to aid me in creating my illustrations in my studio at home. I achieved all my purposes on the trip—though rarely in the exact manner I had planned. India, I quickly learned, will shape and teach the visitor as she wishes.

In Bodh Gaya, the site of Buddha's enlightenment, I made a remarkable find, a late nineteenth-century compilation by E. B. Cromwell of five hundred fifty Jataka tales. During the trip I produced about seventy sketches and took hundreds of photographs that were to prove invaluable in creating the paintings. While extremely demanding and difficult in many ways, my visit was a great success in preparing for this project.

Back in my studio, I began the task of selecting the stories to work with in my series. It was a difficult job, but I finally arrived at forty-four stories that I chose for their moral teachings and visual potential. The older English translations were rather dated and difficult in style, so I decided to retell the stories in a contemporary American voice.

The Buddha used stories such as these to teach his monks how to live together harmoniously and to instruct them in the virtues that were at the core of his teachings. How many of these stories were original creations of the Buddha? How many were traditional folklore? How many were added after his death? We will never know the answers to these questions. We do know the Jatakas are stories that deal with compassion, loving kindness, avoiding trickery, the importance and responsibility of leadership, harmony, the evils of intoxication, ingratitude, greed, the danger of addiction, the certainty of change, the price of deceit, the importance of education, respect and care for elders, tolerance, generosity, false holiness, overcoming fear, the safety of familiar ground, the care needed in delegating duties, the danger of false praise, the consequences of talking too much, the necessity of foresight, the cruelty of hunting, the relative nature of beauty, the joys of friendship, knowing one's limits, and many more themes.

Employing animals to illuminate the basic human condition is a universal device for pointing out human foibles and virtues with clarity and humor; since those qualities remain much as they were two thousand five hundred years ago, these tales remain just as relevant today as they were then. My hope is that you will enjoy these stories and illustrations as much as I enjoyed researching, painting, and bringing them to you.

—MARK W. MCGINNIS

THE BEETLE AND THE ELEPHANT

Long ago there was a riverside inn situated between two Indian towns. Naturally, travelers stayed and dined at the inn, and some would sit outside drinking liquor. One of the drunken travelers spilled his bowl of beer, and the liquid settled into the hollow of a rock. A dung beetle was making his way to the river, being drawn there by the smell of droppings from the traveler's animals. The beetle stumbled across the spilled beer and found it very tasty. He drank his fill and soon he had lost all his good sense. He staggered down to the riverbank and fell over the animal droppings and mud. When he finally got to his feet he sank into the mud. "I am so mighty," said the drunken beetle, "that the world cannot bear my massive weight!"

At just that moment an elephant was making his way to the river for a drink. Seeing the foolish beetle falling about in the animal droppings, the elephant backed up to take another route to the water. The beetle, seeing the elephant's retreat called out to him, "You coward, come back here! I can see that you fear my power. Come back here and fight me!"

The elephant realized the beetle was drunk and decided to teach him a lesson. "I accept your challenge Mr. Beetle," said the Elephant, "and I will choose the weapons of our fight."

So saying the elephant turned, lifted his tail, and covered the beetle in a huge pile of elephant dung. "You are in your element now, Mr. Beetle, and I claim victory." With that the elephant went to the river, took his drink, and returned to the forest, while the foolhardy beetle struggled and struggled under the mound of dung.

THE BUFFALO AND THE MONKEY

THE BUFFALO AND THE MONKEY

Long ago, in a beautiful forest outside the city of Gaya in northeastern India, there lived a mighty bull buffalo. He was a sight to behold— massive, with bulging muscles and huge curving horns with razor sharp tips. He was like a dark blue mountain moving through the forest. The lions and tigers stayed out of his path, for they knew they were no match for his strength.

But the buffalo's nature was the opposite of his appearance. He was the most gentle and wise of creatures. A mischievous monkey had discovered the buffalo's kindness, and he decided to abuse it. The monkey had found that the buffalo would put up with whatever trick he played. The monkey would jump on the bull's back and ride him like a horse, or swing in between his great horns, or cover his eyes so he couldn't find his way; he would stand in his path so he couldn't graze, jump on his head when he was sleeping and wake him, or even poke his ears with a stick. Whatever the monkey did, the buffalo went on about his business, not seeming to mind a bit. The monkey reveled in the situation, always trying to think up new ways to anger the buffalo.

An owl who lived in the woods often observed the monkey and buffalo, and she was very perplexed about the relationship. One day she asked the buffalo, "Great buffalo, you are feared by the tiger and the lion, yet you let this monkey abuse you in countless ways. In an instant you could crush the insolent little beast and be done with him. Why don't you?"

"Of course I know my own strength," said the buffalo, "but I would not think of using it on that silly little monkey. It is very easy to be patient and tolerant of those who are good to you. The challenge is being patient and tolerant with those who treat you badly. This monkey, with his taunting, is actually doing me a favor. I work on developing the virtue of tolerance and compassion by putting up with his behavior. Maybe he will learn from my example, and maybe he won't. It is not my job to discipline him. We all need challenges to develop our virtues. This monkey is supplying me with a chance to grow."

"Your greatness, wondrous buffalo, is not just in your size, but also in your sublime wisdom. Thank you for teaching me this important lesson," said the owl, who then bowed to the buffalo and flew back to the treetops to contemplate his remarkable words.

THE ELEPHANT AND THE DOG

12

THE ELEPHANT AND THE DOG

Long ago in the great city of Varanasi the king kept a stable of elephants. His favorite elephant had an unusual best friend—a dog who first came to the stable to eat the rice that fell from the elephant's mouth as she ate her dinner. As time went on, the elephant and the dog developed a close and loving relationship, until it came to pass that the elephant would not eat unless the dog was there to share her meal. The dog would sleep curled up by the leg of the elephant, would bathe with the elephant, and they would play together, the elephant swinging the dog with her trunk.

One day an unkind stable hand sold the dog to a passing peasant for a few coins. The elephant was miserable. She would not eat, drink, or bathe; she simply stood in her stall, swaying sadly from side to side. When the king was told of the worsening condition of his favorite animal he was very upset. He called in his wisest adviser and told him, "Go to my beloved elephant and find out what is wrong with her."

The adviser went and carefully examined the elephant. He clearly saw that there was nothing physically wrong with the beast, so he concluded that it must be an emotional problem. He asked the elephant's primary caretaker, "Is there anything different in the stables lately?"

The caretaker said, "Why, yes, the elephant had a great friend in a dog, who has vanished recently."

With that the adviser went back to the king and said, "Your elephant is heartbroken at the disappearance of a dog she much loved."

"Well," said the king, "how am I to find a lost dog in this huge city?"

"I recommend putting forth a proclamation declaring that anyone who is found in custody of a dog from the king's elephant stable will be forced to pay a large fine," said the adviser.

So it was done, and as soon as the peasant who had bought the dog heard of the proclamation, he immediately released it, and the dog dashed directly back to the elephant stables.

When the exhausted dog returned, the elephant wept tears of joy, and she scooped the dog up with her trunk and cradled it. She would not eat until the dog had been fed; then she ate her food as well and was soon back to her old ways, her canine friend forever at her side.

THE ALERT ANTELOPE

ong ago in a forest outside the great Indian city of Varanasi lived a beautiful and intelligent antelope who fed on the fruit that fell from trees, harming no other living creature. In the same region of the forest there also dwelled a hunter who, quite the contrary, made his living by slaying the animals of the forest.

The clever hunter found that he could build a platform up in the branches of the great fruit trees and spear animals when they came to eat the fruits that fell below. This would catch the animals unaware, as they were used to looking for predators on the ground and not in the trees.

The hunter found a *sepanni* tree whose ripe fruits were just beginning to fall, and he noticed there were fresh antelope tracks around the tree and other evidence of an animal feeding there. The hunter thought this would be a good spot to build one of his platforms. He got the necessary materials, climbed the tree, and built the platform in an area he thought was well concealed from the animal's sight but would still give the hunter a clear opportunity to hurl his spear at the prey. He built the platform in such a way that he could stand up and throw his spear with all his might and still maintain his balance in the tree.

The hunter was careful to remove any sign that he had been working in the area and the next morning he came very early, before the sun rose, and positioned himself on his sturdy platform. He waited and waited, and his patience was rewarded. Through the trees he could see an antelope making its way to the *sepanni* tree.

This was the same antelope that had been there on previous days. She loved the sweet ripe fruit of the *sepanni* tree and had been feeding at this one for several years. As she approached the tree she caught an unusual scent—not the scent of ripe *sepanni* fruit, but a very slight scent of what might be a human being. She stopped in her tracks and went no further. The hunter saw her pause and wondered what the problem was. He waited for some time, and the antelope also stayed where she was, trying to discern if it was a human scent she had picked up.

The antelope was out of the hunter's range to throw his spear, so he decided to try to bring the antelope closer to the tree. He took some ripe *sepanni* fruit and gently tossed them to the area in front of the antelope.

This was more than enough to convince the antelope that something was wrong, and with her keen eyesight she could discern that there was a man hiding in the foliage of the tree. She decided to make a little jest of the hunter's folly. She said, "Oh great *sepanni* tree, this is most unusual. Whereas your fruit usually falls straight to the ground, today it comes flying out to meet me; and whereas the fruit usually falls only infrequently, today three fall nearly at once, even though there is no wind. Oh great tree, since you have stopped acting like a tree, I will not feed

THE ALERT ANTELOPE

under your branches today, but instead look for a tree that acts like one." She turned and started walking away.

The hunter was furious at being so mocked and rose up on his platform and hurled his spear, which landed ten feet short of its mark, "Begone with you! You have escaped me today, but another day my spear will find its mark!" he screamed at her.

The antelope turned one last time with some words of advice, "Hunter, you might want to reconsider your way of life. Anyone who uses such trickery to slay the gentle creatures of the forest will eventually reap very harsh rewards. Think again about your actions here today."

Long ago in north central India there lived a flock of parakeets in a grove of silk cotton trees atop a hill. The flock was ruled over by a wise king and queen. They also had a beautiful son who became more gorgeous in his plumage and form with each passing year. The king and queen were growing old and no longer had the strength or eyesight to lead the flock. They called their son to their side and told him that he now needed to lead the parakeets to the best feeding sites. The son graciously accepted the duty and told his parents that he would now care for them as they had so lovingly cared for him when he was young.

The area all around the hill on which the parakeets lived was owned by a wealthy landowner who had more than a thousand acres planted in rice. He had divided his fields into fifty-acre sections and hired a man to care for and watch over each section. The rice in the fields at the base of the hill where the parakeets lived was ripening. The young parakeet king saw this and led his flock there to eat. The man hired to look over this field did not like the parakeets eating the rice and tried to chase them away, but each time he approached them, they simply flew to another part of the field. Observing the birds, the caretaker saw something quite unusual: after the largest and most beautiful of the parakeets ate his fill, he gathered up a large quantity of heads of rice in his beak and flew off with them. He had never seen a parakeet gather rice before.

As the parakeets ate more and more rice, the hired man began to worry that the landowner would hold him responsible for the loss. He decided to go to the owner right away and tell him of the problem. The landowner was not overly concerned about the rice eaten by the birds, but he was fascinated by the account of the beautiful parakeet who carried off rice in his beak. He told the hired man to snare the rice-gathering parakeet and bring it to him alive. The hired man was thankful that the landowner was not upset about the damage to his crops and he set a snare in the same area that the parakeet king had been eating the day before.

The next day the parakeet king returned to the same area and unknowingly stepped into the snare. As it tightened around his leg he thought, "If I give the alarm cry it will frighten all the flock away and they will not be able to finish their meal. I will bear the pain until they have eaten and then sound the alarm." And that is what he did. After he judged that the flock had eaten its fill, he gave the alarm cry and all the birds took to the air in fright, leaving him alone in the snare.

The hired man heard the commotion of the panicked birds from his hut and knew something had happened. He hurried to the spot where he had laid the snare. "What luck!" he cried. "This is exactly the bird I wished to capture, and here he is securely in the snare." He tied the parakeet's legs together with a leather strap and carried him to the house of the landowner, who gently took the parakeet in

THE DUTIFUL PARAKEET

his hands and said to the bird, "Beautiful parakeet, why do you fly off with beaks full of my rice? Do you have your own farm? Or possibly you have a granary? Or do you dislike me and wish to punish me?"

The parakeet answered in a kind-hearted voice, "Dear sir, I hold no ill will toward you, and I have no granary or farm. I am simply doing my duty. My parents have grown old and weak of wing and eye, and, out of my love for them, I am bringing back food for them as they did so many times for me when I was young."

The landowner was deeply moved by the parakeet's love and kindness toward his elderly parents. "What noble and blessed thoughts come from you, dear bird," said the owner as he removed the straps that bound the parakeet's legs together and rubbed healing oils into the wounds caused by the snare. He then fed the parakeet sweet parched corn and sugar water. On releasing the parakeet king, the landowner said, "Fly back to your flock and your parents. You and your flock are welcome to eat from any of my fields whenever you wish. You have shown me how a good son truly loves and respects his parents."

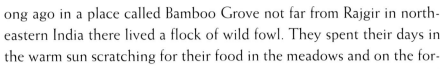

THE FALCON AND THE WILD FOWL

Long ago in a place called Bamboo Grove not far from Rajgir in north-eastern India there lived a flock of wild fowl. They spent their days in the warm sun scratching for their food in the meadows and on the forest floors. Then into their region came a powerful falcon. He was a great and speedy hunter, and whenever the fowl ventured into the open he would swoop down like lightening, grab one with his great talons, and consume the victim for his dinner. This went on until nearly half the flock was gone. The leader of the flock, a wise rooster, decided they needed to change their habits if they were to survive. He kept what was left of the flock always within the bamboo grove, where the density of bamboo stalks and foliage made it impossible for the fast-flying falcon to take even one more bird.

The falcon observed and understood the rooster's fine leadership, but he thought that perhaps he could trick the rooster out into the open and dine on him. The rest of the birds, without the rooster's wise counsel, would soon be his as well.

The falcon flew near the bamboo grove, lit on a branch of a tree, and called out to the rooster, "Most worthy fowl, I have been observing your noble ways and great influence on the flock. Do not fear me. I wish to be your friend. I know a place near here that has the most succulent seeds for our taking. Come with me and we can eat together as companions."

"No, great hunter," said the rooster. "Between you and I there can be no friendship. Go away. I have no need of your companionship."

"But good sir," pleaded the falcon, "I am a changed bird. I am no longer a hunter of fowl but wish to be their friend and protector. Give me a chance to prove myself true."

The rooster replied, "These are things that I have heard and believe—'Trust not those whose words are lies, or those who only show self-interest, or those who seem to be too devout. Trust not those of a changeable mind, as they are likely to change their mind again. Trust not those with violent ways, as that violence may be turned against you. Trust not smooth words that do not come from the heart, as they will deceive you.' All this teaches me not to trust you, falcon. As long as you are in this region my flock and I will stay in these safe bamboo groves where there is plenty to eat and we can keep our lives secure."

Seeing that the rooster was much too wise to be fooled, the falcon took to wing and flew far away to look for a hunting ground populated by less cautious birds.

THE FEARFUL ELEPHANT

THE FEARFUL ELEPHANT

ong ago, a beautiful elephant lived in the forest outside the capital of an Indian kingdom south of the great Himalaya Mountains. She was a large, strong, young elephant with skin so light it might be called white. She enjoyed her life in the forest with her mother and the rest of the herd and had a kind, but timid, personality.

One day her beauty and size came to the attention of the king's elephant trainers, and they decided to capture and train her for the king's pleasure. The king's trainers, riding their large bull elephants, seized her, placed a huge rope around her neck, and brought her to the training ground. She was then forced into a pen made of logs, and the trainers poked and beat her from the outside of the pen in an attempt to break her will and make her do as they wished. While this technique worked for many elephants, it terrified the beautiful young elephant. Each time the trainers came she panicked, smashing against the sides of her pen. One day in her frightened rage she broke down the pen and fled.

In her frenzy the white elephant ran into the valleys of the great Himalayas. She ran and ran until she was deep in the mountains, far beyond where people usually went. The king's men were instructed to bring her back, but after many attempts to find her they finally gave up the hunt. Although she was in complete safety deep in the mountains, she was still as fearful as she was in her pen. The slightest sound— the wind in the trees or the snap of a twig—would cause her to run through the forest in a panicked state, swinging her great trunk from side to side. She spent most of her time crashing through the mountain valleys in terror. A wise owl who lived in the same valleys often watched the poor beast fleeing her own shadow and felt a deep compassion for the creature's miserable condition. One day the owl flew down and lit on a branch close to the elephant. The elephant was about to run away when the owl said, "Great beast, do not fear. I am only a small bird and I wish you no harm." With that the elephant delayed its flight and listened to the owl, who continued: "You have nothing to fear from me, you have nothing to fear from the wind, you have nothing to fear from anything in this forest. You are the greatest of beings here. There are no men about. Your fear is controlling you. You have created the fear and now the fear is destroying you. You can also end your fear with your own mind. You have the power to control your thoughts."

The elephant listened intently to the owl's sensible words and responded, "Kind and wise owl, you have opened my eyes and my mind to my behavior. Thank you for caring about me." From that day on, little by little, the elephant began to control her fear. When she heard an unfamiliar noise, instead of bolting away in fear she stopped to think about what the sound was, and reminded herself not to be afraid.

The Woodpecker and the Lion

Long ago in a forest in northwest India there lived a woodpecker who was very unusual for both his great beauty and his behavior. While most woodpeckers eat insects and worms, this woodpecker could not bear to take the life of another living creature, so instead he ate the young shoots of plants, flowers, and fruits. He also had the reputation among all the animals of the forest of being exceptionally kind and always willing to help others.

One day he was flying through the woods when he heard moaning and groaning coming from below. He flew lower to find a lion lying on its side, gasping and whimpering. Landing on a branch near the lion, the woodpecker said, "Oh great king of beasts, what can be the matter with you? Have you been shot by a poison arrow, or are you ill?" The lion replied, "Oh, kind bird, it is none of those things. I have a sharp bone lodged in my throat. It is causing my throat to swell shut and I will soon die. I cannot swallow it or cough it up. Please, help me if you can."

The woodpecker thought for a moment and then found a sturdy stick on the ground nearby. He asked the lion to open his mouth as wide as possible, and then he lodged the stick between the lion's upper and lower teeth. With the lion's huge, fearsome mouth propped open, the bird flew down his throat to where the bone was securely fixed. The woodpecker carefully worked on one end of the bone and then the other until it gradually began to loosen. Finally, the bone was free, and the woodpecker took it in his beak and flew out of the lion's mouth. He removed the stick and the lion gave a huge sigh of relief. The lion briefly thanked the woodpecker and slunk off to a quiet place to recover from his painful experience. The woodpecker was happy to have been of help and flew off to search for green shoots and fruit.

Some months later, the seasonal rains failed to come and a severe drought afflicted the area where the woodpecker lived. All the fresh shoots on the plants withered and all the blossoms and fruits dried up. The woodpecker was without food for days and days. He grew weaker and weaker and was very close to starvation. As he flew weakly about in search of food, he looked down and saw the same lion he had previously saved from death. It was feeding on an antelope. Since the antelope was already dead, the woodpecker reasoned that it would be all right if he ate a bit of its flesh in order to save his own life. He flew down, and not wanting to seem bold, simply walked back and forth in front of the lion waiting, for an invitation to join him, but no invitation came. Eventually his hunger overcame his modesty and, thinking that the lion must not recognize him, the woodpecker said, "Oh, kind sir, I come to you today like a beggar requesting a few bites to eat that I may not perish from starvation." The lion looked up from his kill and glowered at the bird, "How dare you come this close to me? You have the good fortune of being the

THE WOODPECKER AND THE LION

only creature to have ever been in a lion's mouth and come out alive. That is more than enough. Be gone with you or you will be part of my meal as well!"

The woodpecker felt humiliated at the lion's rejection and flew up to a branch high on a tree overhead. There sat an owl who had been observing the scene and knew of the woodpecker's previous service to the lion. The owl said, "Why do you let that ungrateful creature insult you after all you have done for him? Fly down there and peck out his eyes, or at least take some of meat, which you could easily do with your speed."

The woodpecker replied, "Do not speak like that. It is not my place to punish such behavior. I didn't help him desiring a favor in return; that would have only been a loan, not a true act of mercy."

The owl then said, "You are truly a bird of great compassion and wisdom. I will remember your lesson well." Saddened by the lion's ingratitude but with neither hostility nor vengeance in his heart, the woodpecker flew off to seek food elsewhere.

THE PANICKED RABBIT

ong ago in the countryside outside the city of Mumbai on the west coast of India there lived a rabbit. He had a comfortable den in the roots of a palm tree that was surrounded by large coconut trees. One day after feeding he stretched out next to his den and was daydreaming in his typically foolish way. He thought to himself, "What in the world would I do if the earth were destroyed?" Just as he had that thought, a large coconut fruit dropped from a great height and came down hard on a palm leaf right behind him. It shook the ground with a loud thump. The rabbit immediately thought, "Oh no, my thought has come true! The earth is collapsing!" And without even looking behind him, he started running in a complete panic. As he blindly ran on another rabbit ran up beside him and said, "What is happening? Are you being chased by a jackal?" "No!" said the terrified rabbit, "The earth is breaking apart. Run for your life!" They were quickly joined by dozens of other rabbits, and the news spread until at least fifty rabbits were charging along. The panic then spread to the deer, and then to the boars, and then to the buffalo. They were then joined by an elephant and a rhinoceros and soon hundreds of animals were now blindly charging across the plain heading for the ocean.

In his den high on a hill a great lion heard the stampede approaching and came out to see what was happening. From his high vantage point he saw an incredible scene: a huge herd of every sort of creature stampeding in panic toward the sea. He could also see that nothing was pursing them. Something, he thought, was terribly wrong. He quickly positioned himself in front of the stampede and emitted three blood-curdling roars, which stopped the panicking animals in their tracks.

The lion approached the elephant and asked what was going on. The elephant breathlessly said, "The earth is coming to an end!"

The lion said, "How do you know this?"

"The buffalo told me," gasped the elephant.

The lion went among the buffalo and they all said, "Yes, the earth is collapsing! The deer told us."

The lion went among the deer and they said, "The earth is most certainly breaking up. The rabbits told us."

Talking to the rabbits, the lion finally discovered the rabbit who had begun the great stampede. "How do you know the earth is collapsing?" asked the lion.

The rabbit replied, "I was sitting by my den and heard the earth breaking up right behind me and I ran for my life."

The story sounded very implausible to the lion, so he told the other animals to wait where they were and he would find out if the earth was truly coming to an end. He put the rabbit on in his back and bounded back to the place where the

THE PANICKED RABBIT

rabbit had been. When they arrived the rabbit was so frightened he refused to go near the spot. He timidly pointed it out saying, "Yonder is the place of the most dreadful sound."

The lion inspected the sight and immediately discerned what had happened. The large coconut was still sitting on the broken palm leaf, undoubtedly the source of the sound of the end of the world.

He returned to the animals with the rabbit riding on his back and explained what had happened. The earth was most certainly not coming to an end and it was safe for them to return to their homes. Many felt foolish for blindly following the herd and not using their own good sense to find out what was really happening. Had the lion not been there to stop them they may have run into the sea and drowned in their frenzy.

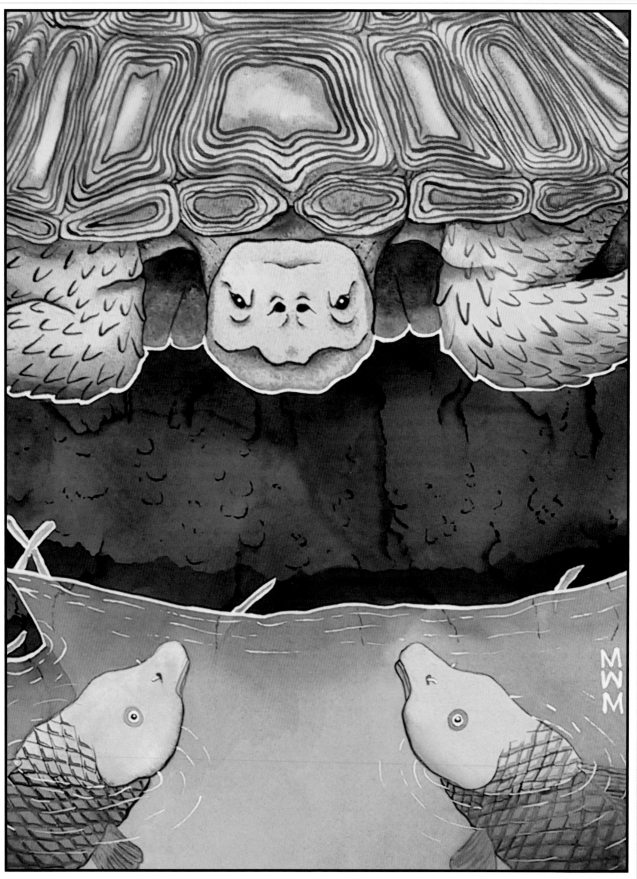

THE FISH AND THE TORTOISE

30

THE FISH AND THE TORTOISE

ong ago outside the great city of Varanasi, where the Ganges River and Jumna River come together, two fish met.

The Ganges fish said to the Jumna fish, "You are a most attractive fish." The Jumna fish replied, "Thank you. You too are certainly a beautiful fish."

"But," said the Ganges fish, "as all know, the fish of the Ganges are always more beautiful than the fish of the Jumna."

"You must be joking!" said the Jumna fish. "It is well known that the fish of the Jumna are vastly more attractive and desirable than the fish of the Ganges. And I am certainly a fine example of that."

"Outrageous!" replied the Ganges fish, "You, more attractive than me? That is absurd."

So the argument as to who was the most beautiful fish went on with no resolution in sight. Finally the two fish saw an old tortoise sunning himself on a rock by the riverside. They decided to take the question to him.

"Excuse us, wise elder tortoise," they said. "We are having a dispute that we cannot resolve. Please help by stating which of us is the most beautiful."

The old tortoise looked at them both very thoughtfully and carefully and then replied, "Jumna and Ganges fish are both certainly very fine. But, for true beauty I would look for a tapering neck, four firm feet, a body round like a spreading Banyan tree, small round eyes, and richly textured, wrinkled skin. Yes, I would have to say that to find true beauty you would have to use me as the example."

"You rascal!" declared the fish. "You have not answered our question but only dwelt on yourself, whom we both find quite ugly. You are of no help at all." Concluding that no resolution was possible when it came to the nature of beauty, they gave up their argument and went their separate ways.

THE FOOLHARDY CROWS

THE FOOLHARDY CROWS

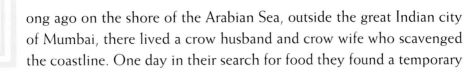

Long ago on the shore of the Arabian Sea, outside the great Indian city of Mumbai, there lived a crow husband and crow wife who scavenged the coastline. One day in their search for food they found a temporary altar that had been used to make offerings to the sea gods. On it were the remains of milk, rice, meat, and strong liquor. The crows eagerly ate and drank it all. They both soon found themselves very drunk from the liquor. They staggered down to the waterline, where they saw sea birds swimming in the surf.

The husband said to the wife, "These sea birds think they are so smart swimming in the surf. We too could swim like that if we wished." "Absolutely!" declared the wife. With all their common sense lost to the liquor, they both waded out into the water and began to feebly paddle about, laughing and bobbing in the water. Suddenly, from out of nowhere, a shark emerged and took the wife in one bite.

The husband, terrified, just managed to make his way back to the shore. Sitting in a stupor on the beach, he bewailed the loss of his beloved wife. "I have lost my wonderful wife to the cruel sea!" he sobbed over and over in a loud, forlorn voice. A large crowd of crows began to gather around to find out what the commotion was all about. The husband told them the sad story, omitting the truth about being so drunk that they had foolishly gone out into the sea, of which they knew nothing.

The crowd of crows felt very sorry for the husband, and one rather dimwitted crow had an idea. He proposed that they empty the sea by drinking it dry, thereby liberating the wife from the watery depths. The other crows thought it worth a try and they all began drinking and drinking. They drank until their mouths were sore and inflamed from the salt water and their jaws ached and their throats felt as if they were swelling shut. They finally fell back on the sand. One crow said, "For every bit of water we remove, the sea refills itself just as rapidly. We are making no headway on emptying the sea at all!" The others agreed, and abandoning their attempt to rescue the crow's wife, they began instead to praise her by remembering her great beauty, her fine figure, her lush complexion, and her gorgeous eyes. Before their exaggerated tribute reached its climax, however, a dark storm cloud hanging over the coast let loose a blinding lightning flash and deafening clap of thunder, frightening all the foolhardy crows away.

THE GOLDEN MALLARD

THE GOLDEN MALLARD

Long ago in a forest in northeastern India there lived a golden mallard. He was a spectacular bird. His feathers were not simply gold in color— they were actual gold, catching the light and sparkling with a radiant glory that followed him wherever he went. Knowing how humans lusted after gold, the mallard kept himself well concealed from their sight.

In the area of the forest where he spent most of his time, there was a small hut where a widowed woman lived with her two daughters. The mallard often watched the family and grew very fond of the girls, who were kind and gentle, but also very poor.

One day when the two girls were outside the hut he flew up and landed on the roof. The girls were overjoyed to see such a beautiful bird and called to their mother, "Mother! Come and see the wonderful bird that has landed on our roof!" The mother came out and was equally amazed.

The mallard spoke to them, "I would like to help you in your poverty by giving you one of my feathers occasionally, which you may sell to buy food and clothing." And he plucked out one of his long flight feathers and gave it to one of the girls. The family was delighted, and over the following months the mallard returned and gave them more feathers. The wealth of the household increased greatly; they were now able to afford as much food as they wished, and the mother and girls dressed in beautiful new saris.

One day the mother said to the girls, "I don't know if we can trust that bird. What if one day he decides never to return? We won't have the money to buy all the wonderful things we have now. I think we should catch the mallard the next time he comes and pluck out all his feathers. Then we will be the richest family in the land."

The girls protested strongly, thinking of the pain it would cause the kind bird. But the next time the golden mallard came to offer them one of his feathers, the mother seized him. She furiously pulled out all his long golden feathers and threw him into a large barrel. But then something amazing happened. All the feathers she had plucked slowly changed to regular gray and tan mallard feathers. It was like watching the color of life go out of something that had died. In cruelly stealing the feathers, the mother had deprived them of their magic and beauty.

The mother wailed and lamented the loss of the great fortune she thought she would have, but the girls wept for the poor mallard. He could not fly, but he was still alive and the girls carefully nursed him back to health, giving him their own food. In time he grew new feathers—but not gold, only ordinary gray and tan.

When his health was renewed and his feathers grown back, he flew away to live his life with a flock of mallards deep in the forest. He was sorry to leave the love and kindness of the girls and promised to visit them from time to time, but he no longer wished to live near human society, for he had seen what greed can do.

THE HAWK AND THE PARTRIDGE

THE HAWK AND THE PARTRIDGE

Long ago a young partridge lived in the cultivated fields outside the great city of Varanasi, where he found his food by hopping about on the plowed clods of earth, eating the tasty morsels turned up by the farmer's labor. The clods were soft when freshly plowed, but the hot Indian sun soon dried them rock-hard.

The partridge's family had always gleaned the fields for their food, and his father had taught him how to find the best seeds and be careful in his feeding. One day the young partridge grew tired of all the hopping about he had to do in the hot sun. He remembered hearing that at the edge of the forest there was shade from the sun's heat and many luscious seeds to eat, and off he flew. Sure enough, there he found an abundance of seeds and cool shade from the towering trees. He ate with such enthusiasm he did not notice a hawk perched high on a bare branch at the forest's edge, where he could clearly see all that went on below. The hawk, however, was paying attention. He took to the air, gained some height, and then silently swooped down, lifting the unsuspecting partridge up into the air in the steel grip of his sharp talons. He was flying the partridge to his favorite perch, where he intended to eat him for supper.

In a loud voice, so the hawk would be sure to hear, the partridge said, "What a fool I have been. I should have never come here to feed. It was a stupid mistake. If I had stayed on my familiar ground this hawk wouldn't have had a chance of catching me."

He could hear the hawk chuckling in his arrogance so he continued, "Yes, if I had been in my domain I would have been more than an equal in a fight with this great bird."

Now the hawk was laughing outright, and he said to the partridge, "Now where would it be that a partridge is the equal of a hawk!"

"In the open plowed field where my father taught me how to feed, Great Hawk," replied the partridge.

"You, a match for me in an open field!" howled the hawk, "This I must see for myself. I will release you and we shall have our match in the field."

With that the hawk released his grip on the partridge who took to wing and flew directly to the plowed field where he usually fed. He landed on an immense, stone-like clod of dirt that had a good-sized overhang behind it.

The hawk was circling overhead and the partridge called, "I am ready for you Mr. Hawk." The hawk dove with all its might at the bold little partridge standing straight and tall on the large, hard dirt clod. The partridge stood firm until the moment before the hawk made contact, then jumped back and under the clod. The mighty hawk crashed into the hard clod with such impact that it knocked him unconscious.

With that the partridge hopped back on the clod and said, "It is true what my father always told me: we are always safest on familiar ground."

 THE IGNORANT MONKEYS

Long ago in the pleasure park of the king of Varanasi there lived a happy troop of monkeys. They had a very good life, with all the food they could eat and no worries about their safety. One day the gardener of the park decided he wanted to go to a week-long festival in the city, but he had just planted some young trees that needed to be watered in four day's time. It occurred to the gardener that even monkeys could do a job as simple as watering trees, and he decided to ask them for help while he was at the festival.

The gardener went to the leader of the monkeys and, after reminding him how lucky the monkeys were to be living in the park, asked if they would do the watering. The leader said they would be happy to help. Reassured, the gardener left the monkeys with watering pots and went off to the festival.

The monkey leader kept careful track of the time, and in four days he called all the monkeys together, gave them the watering pots, and told them to water the trees. The monkeys began wildly running around sprinkling and splashing water on the trees' leaves, with the result that little water actually reached the ground. The leader knew that the water should be applied to the trees' roots, but he was uncertain how much they needed. He then called all the monkeys together again and told them, "In order to know how much water to give the young trees, let us pull each tree out of the ground and see if it has long roots or short roots. We'll give more water to those with long roots, and less to those whose roots are short."

"A brilliant idea," said the other monkeys, and off they went, uprooting every young tree that the gardener had planted.

Of course, it didn't matter how much water they gave the roots. The young trees were in such shock from being uprooted that most began to die immediately.

Two of the king's advisers were strolling through the park and observed the strange behavior of the monkeys. One of the advisors stopped a monkey who was uprooting a tree and asked him what he thought he was doing. The monkey eagerly told them, "The gardener has asked us to help with the watering in his absence, and we are following the orders of our great leader to water the trees according to their root length."

The adviser turned to his companion and said, "This is a fine example of how good intentions can be disastrous when carried out by those of little knowledge or wisdom."

The second adviser responded, "How true. And you certainly have to question the intelligence of a gardener who asks monkeys to perform such a task in the first place."

THE IGNORANT MONKEYS

THE JACKAL AND THE CROW

THE JACKAL AND THE CROW

ong ago on the outskirts of the great city of Varanasi there was a beautiful grove of rose-apple trees. Their fruit was ripe, and a crow was sitting on a lower branch of one of the trees enjoying the sweet apples. A jackal who was prowling through the grove looking for anything he might eat spied the crow feasting on the fruit, which was far out of his reach.

The jackal thought, "Crows are known to have a vain nature. If I flatter this bird, maybe he will throw some of the delicious fruit down to me."

He began loudly, "What is that I hear up in that tree? It sounds like the fairest songbird I have ever heard. Such a sweet song and gentle cooing—why, it melts my heart. And now I can see this wonderful creature's appearance. It is more marvelous than a peacock, with lustrous features, rich color, and a fine form. It is most certainly noble in breeding and birth. This is the most magnificent bird I have ever seen!"

The crow preened and puffed himself up as he listened to the jackal's lies. When the jackal had finished the crow replied, "It certainly does take one of noble birth to recognize another. You yourself have the bearing and beauty of a young tiger. Here, let me share some this fine fruit with you." With that the crow shook the branch and a shower of fruit rained down on the wily jackal, fulfilling his well-laid plan.

An owl sitting in a nearby tree, who had witnessed the entire exchange, shook her head and said, "These two creatures are scavengers and eaters of garbage and the dead, the lowest of the birds and the lowest of the animals, flattering and lying to one another. While the fruit around me is sweet, this scene is enough to turn my stomach." And she flew off to another part of the forest.

GRANNY'S BLACKIE

GRANNY'S BLACKIE

Long ago in a small village outside the great city of Varanasi lived a poor old widow. Her brother had once done a favor for a wealthy man in the city and as a reward he presented rare gifts to all the brother's family. The unusual gift he gave to the old woman was a baby elephant. The old woman was delighted and treated the elephant as if he were her own child. She fed it rice and porridge and worked hard to make enough money to feed the increasing appetite of the growing elephant.

The elephant became a member of the village and was especially loved by the children, for whom he was a constant playmate. The children called him Granny's Blackie because of his unusual dark color. Blackie would give them rides, swing them with his trunk, and spray them with water when they played at the river.

One day Blackie said to Granny, "Please come with me to the river today." She answered, "Oh, Blackie, I would like to but I have far too much work today." For the first time it occurred to Blackie how hard the old woman worked to support the two of them while he, now a full-grown elephant, played all day with the children. He thought to himself, "I must be on the lookout for some work so Granny will not have to work so hard."

The next day he was down at the river with the children when a caravan owner came to the riverbank with five hundred carts he was trying to transport to Varanasi. The carts were heavily loaded with goods, and the caravan owner's oxen could not pull them across the rough river bottom even at its shallowest place. He needed to get the merchandise to the city soon or he would lose a great deal of money. The caravan owner saw the elephant by the river with the children and asked, "Who owns this great beast?" The children said, "He belongs to an old widow in the village whom we call Granny, and his name is Blackie."

"Well," said the man, "I will pay Blackie two coins for every cart he can pull across the river." Hearing this, Blackie was delighted, as he knew that would be enough money for Granny and he to live on for some time. One by one he pulled the carts across the rough river bottom. It was very hard work, but he was strong and he endured. He pulled all five hundred carts across the river.

The caravan owner went to his wagon and came back with a bag of five hundred coins, which he tied around the elephant's neck. Blackie felt the weight of the bag and knew that it did not contain the one thousand coins that he had been promised. He walked to the front of the caravan and lay down. Try as they would, they could not get the elephant move. The owner finally realized that the elephant knew he was being cheated. He removed the bag from around Blackie's neck, took it to his wagon, and added the five hundred coins. He then tied the bag back on Blackie, who immediately rose and let the caravan pass.

Blackie headed straight for home, the children running along beside him. He was tired, covered with dust and mud, and his eyes were bloodshot from the strain of his labors. When Granny saw him in such a state she said, "Oh, Blackie, where have you been, and how did you come to such a state? What is that hanging around your neck?"

The children told her the entire story of the hard work Blackie had done and how he would not move until he had been paid the price originally offered. Granny was very proud of Blackie, and she and the children led him back to river, where they bathed him and scrubbed him clean. That evening Granny made Blackie an extra portion of his favorite food. From that day on Blackie continued to get occasional jobs that brought in enough money for the old woman and he to live comfortably, and Granny lived out her remaining years in ease.

THE MOTHER MOUSE

Long ago in an abandoned village a few miles from Varanasi in north-west India a Mother Mouse lived in a long-deserted house. The house had belonged to a wealthy merchant who stored a fortune in gold coins under the floor; he died without ever telling a soul about his hidden treasure. The mouse had found the gold, but being a mouse, had little use for it, and she went about her business as usual, hunting for her daily food.

On the outskirts of the village was an old stone quarry that was still in use by a single stonecutter. He was a kind, gentle young man, and the mouse observed him often and thought what a good and compassionate person he seemed to be. One day she remembered the great fortune of gold hidden in her house, and she decided to share it with the stonecutter. The next day she took one gold coin in her mouth and brought it to the young man.

The stonecutter looked down at the mouse holding the gold coin in her mouth and asked with amazement, "Mother Mouse, what have brought for me?!"

She replied, "I have brought you a gold coin for your own use—and perhaps you would also be kind enough to buy a little meat for me as well."

"I would be most happy to," said the stonecutter and he spent a small portion of the gold's worth on a considerable piece of meat for the mouse.

This transaction continued day after day, with the mouse bringing the stone-cutter a gold coin and the stonecutter supplying the mouse with meat. But one day disaster struck. A cat caught Mother Mouse.

"Please, don't eat me," pleaded the mouse. "It would be a mistake!"

"A mistake?" replied the cat. "How could it be a mistake for a cat to eat a mouse? That is what cats do, and I am very hungry."

"May I ask you," said Mother Mouse, "are you hungry just today, or are you hungry every day?"

"I am hungry every day, of course," said the cat.

"If you eat me now, you will satisfy your hunger for today. But if you let me live I will give you meat every day, and your hunger will satisfied for many days," said the mouse.

"Well," said the cat, "I will let you live, but you had better live up to your end of the bargain."

So the mouse divided her portion of meat that the stonecutter brought daily and gave the cat half. Her luck, however, remained bad, for she was caught by a second cat. She ended up making the same arrangement, now splitting the meat three ways. Then a third cat caught her, and the meat was split so many ways that there was nearly none left for her. She grew thinner and thinner until she was only skin and bones.

The stonecutter grew concerned over her appearance and said, "Mother, are you ill? I bring you food every day, and yet you are so thin." In her exhausted state the mouse told him the entire sad story.

"Mother Mouse," said the stonecutter, "you should have told me this long ago. I can help you."

The stonecutter took a block of the finest crystal and worked and polished it until it was a transparent mass as clear as air. He then carved a chamber down into the middle of the mass and polished it until it, too, was invisible. The stonecutter set the crystal block in Mother Mouse's old house, where the cats always came to claim their share of the meat, placing Mother Mouse down inside the chamber. He positioned the block very carefully, so that light would not reflect off the surface of the block and only the mouse would be visible. He then instructed the mouse that when the cats came for their meat, she was to insult the cats and make them angry.

When the first cat came he said, "Mouse, where is my meat? I am very hungry today."

The mouse said, "Why don't you go eat some leaves? I am tired of supplying a free-loading creature like you with food."

This infuriated the cat. "I won't be eating leaves today. I will be eating mouse!" he cried as he leapt with all his might at the mouse, completely unaware of the crystal block surrounding her. He slammed into the surface of the rock with such an impact that he was dazed to near unconsciousness; when he regained his senses he was gripped with terror at the supernatural powers of the mouse, and he dashed out of the house, never to return.

In a little while the second cat came for his portion of the meat. "Where is my supper, Mother Mouse? I don't see it anywhere," he demanded.

"I decided you could supply me with my supper tonight instead, you mangy alley cat," said the mouse confidently.

The second cat bared its teeth and said, "I know what I will be having for supper." And with his mouth wide open, he dove at the mouse. His teeth struck the surface of the crystal, cracked, and he fled with blood pouring from his mouth. The third cat also came for his meat and met a similar fate. All three cats were convinced that the mouse had great powers, and they wanted nothing more to do with her.

The stonecutter returned and removed Mother Mouse from the chamber in the crystal. She was so grateful to the young man that she showed him where all the gold coins had been hidden in the house. The awestruck man took the gold and the mouse to his home where they lived in friendship, happiness, and great comfort for the rest of their years.

THE MONKEY AND THE CROCODILE

Long ago in a jungle to the south of Varanasi there was a quick-witted, wonderful monkey. He lived alone along a beautiful stretch of a river. In the middle of the river was an island where the best fruit trees to be found anywhere grew. To reach the island the monkey would take a huge leap to a solitary rock that was in the middle of the river, and then another leap to the island with the sweet fruits. He usually visited the island in the morning and returned to his home each evening.

Also in that stretch of the river lived a pair of crocodiles. The female had watched the monkey day after day and decided she wanted to make a meal of the strong, plump creature. She begged her mate to bring her the monkey as a gift, and after much nagging he reluctantly promised to do so.

His plan was to rest his huge head on top of the rock in mid-river that the monkey always leapt to on the way to the island, and wait for the monkey to jump into his mouth. The crocodile waited until evening, when the monkey would be returning from the island and the light would be dim and shadowy, concealing his form.

The monkey ate his fill and, as the sun was setting, decided it was time to make his way home. As he was getting ready to make his leap to the stone in the middle of the river, he noticed that the stone seemed higher in the river than he had ever seen it. He knew that the river level had not changed, so something must be wrong. He decided to try a test and called, "Mr. Rock, oh, Mr. Rock, how are you tonight?" The crocodile remained silent. "Mr. Rock, my friend, why don't you answer me tonight?" continued the monkey.

"Well," thought the crocodile, "if the rock usually answers the monkey I had better do so." He said aloud, "Hello my fine monkey friend, how are you this lovely evening?"

"I'm just fine," said the monkey knowingly, "but you most surely are not a rock. Who are you and what do you want?"

"I am a crocodile," replied the rock impersonator, "and I have been sent by my wife who wishes to have you for dinner."

The monkey responded, "Well, as it seems to be my fate, I can see no other way than to give myself up to you. Open your mouth wide and I will jump into it."

The monkey knew that when crocodiles open their mouths they must close their eyes, making them blind to the world. The monkey took a great leap and landed not in the reptile's gaping mouth but on the back of his head and quickly made the second bound to the river bank before the crocodile could make a move.

The monkey turned to the dazed and disappointed crocodile and said, "Your wife will have to find a different meal tonight." And he went on his way. The crocodile slowly made his way back to his home, not looking forward to telling his mate that he could not keep his promise.

THE MONKEY AND THE CROCODILE

THE MONKEY AND THE PEAS

Long ago at the king's stables in the great city of Varanasi there was a monkey who spent a great deal of time in a tree above a trough where the king's favorite horses were fed. One day the trough was filled with steamed peas for the horses. The monkey loved peas. He scampered down the tree, filled his mouth and hands with peas, and made his way back up the tree.

As he sat eating his treasure, one pea dropped from his hand down to the ground below. The monkey panicked at the loss of the pea and scrambled down the tree dropping all his other peas on the way. He looked and looked for the lost pea but could not find it. By the time he had given up hope the horses had eaten not only all the peas from the trough but also all of the peas the monkey had dropped. The monkey slowly climbed back up the tree and sat with a tragically forlorn look on his face.

The stable hands who had been watching the incident laughed and laughed at the monkey's misfortune. The king and his closest adviser, who had come to inspect the horses, also witnessed the misadventure of the poor creature. The king asked his adviser, "My dear friend, what do you make of that?"

The adviser responded, "Your Majesty, this is a commonly observed event. How many men have lost a thousand coins trying to save one? How many kings have lost kingdoms trying to save something of paltry importance?"

The king nodded his head and said, "How true. Foolishness is not confined to monkeys. It can be as easily found in men—whether peasants or kings."

THE OTTERS AND THE JACKAL

The Otters and the Jackal

ong ago in a small but beautiful river that led to the great Ganges in northeastern India, there lived two otters who hunted, swam, and played. A short distance from the river was a den that was the home to two jackals who lived by scavenging up and down the river for whatever they could find to eat.

On a fine summer day, one of the otters was hunting in the river and managed to latch onto a great rohita fish. The fish was so large that it began swimming away with the otter, but he managed to call to his mate for help, and between the two of them, they finally landed the huge fish. At first they lay there in complete exhaustion, but when they finally caught their breath they began talking about how to divide the fish between themselves. The discussion quickly developed into an argument, and it was soon evident that no decision could be reached.

Just then the male jackal wandered down the riverbank looking for food. The otters were glad to see him and said, "Esteemed Jackal, please help us settle this dispute, as we cannot determine how to divide this great fish between the two of us."

The jackal put on his most dignified appearance and in a stately voice said, "You have chosen the right animal for such a case. I have dealt with many similar problems and I have always concluded them peacefully."

He asked them the circumstances and details of the capture of the fish, and then he very carefully studied it. Abruptly he said to the otter on his left, "You take the head," and to the otter on his right he said, "You take the tail." Both otters complied with the jackal's order and waited further divisions.

The jackal then said, "I will take the middle as my fee for settling this dispute," and in a flash he grabbed the huge middle section of the fish and was gone.

The two outwitted otters stood there, one with the head in his mouth and the other with the tail. The one holding the tail dropped it and said, "If we had both not been so greedy, we would still have that fine meal."

The second otter dropped the fish head and replied, "It is a lesson I will not soon forget."

Meanwhile the jackal brought the huge piece of fish into his den where his mate was waiting.

THE PARAKEETS AND THE MONKEY

THE PARAKEETS AND THE MONKEY

Long ago in a forest outside the ancient Indian city of Varanasi lived two beautiful parakeets who were brothers. The older brother was well known for his wisdom, while the younger brother still had much to learn. They were both glorious birds to see, with brilliant plumage and perfectly formed bodies.

A local hunter had seen the birds often and decided to capture and present them to the king in the city. It was a difficult task, but the hunter was persistent and he finally snared both birds.

The king was exceedingly pleased with the gorgeous parakeets and gave the hunter a large reward. The great ruler had a golden cage built for the birds. They were fed the finest grains and honey and given sugar water to drink from silver bowls. The king spent much time speaking to the parakeets and they soon became favorites of the entire court.

But the parakeets' good fortune was to change. A woodsman heard of the generous reward the king gave the hunter for the parakeets, so he trapped and tamed a large black monkey, which he then presented to the king. Again, the king was delighted and rewarded the woodsman handsomely. The court very quickly shifted its attention to the monkey, which made funny faces and entertained them with his comical antics. The monkey was given the most delicious foods and a bed of silk cushions, while the parakeets were rarely talked to or even looked at. Their food also changed to common grain and ordinary water.

The younger parakeet brother was very upset with this change in fortune. He tried to convince his older brother to escape with him and return to the forest, saying, "We deserve better treatment than this! We were the favorites, not that monkey!" The older brother, however, replied, "Gain and loss, praise and blame, pleasure and pain, fame and dishonor—these are all temporary states. They all change. They persist for a time and then something else takes their place. So it was with us, and so it will be with the monkey."

And so it was with the monkey. He soon became bored with his life at court and amused himself by frightening the king's children, shaking his ears at them and baring his teeth in a menacing fashion. The monkey thought it was very funny, but the children were terrified, and soon they would not even enter the room where the monkey was kept. They complained to the king the monkey had been scaring them, and that they were afraid he was going to bite them. The king became angry and ordered that the monkey be sent back deep into the forest.

So the court's attention returned to the parakeets and they were again given their rich foods and talked to and played with. The younger brother was delighted and said to the older brother, "See, we have regained our proper place at court and been given the attention we deserve." The older brother, whose behavior had not changed a bit through good treatment and bad, only smiled at his brother and said, "Enjoy yourself now, for this too will change."

THE BANYAN DEER

THE BANYAN DEER

Long ago to the north of the great ancient Indian city of Varanasi was an area known for its fine herds of deer. It is now called Sarnath. A beautiful and wise buck known as the Banyan king ruled one herd. He was a brilliant gold color with antlers like polished marble, hooves like polished black ebony, and eyes like two round emeralds. He was well loved by the entire herd. A nearby herd was ruled by a deer known as the Branch king. He was also a beautiful golden deer, and he often came to the Banyan king for counsel and advice.

The king of Varanasi was a wise ruler in most matters, but he did have one weakness: he loved to eat fresh meat everyday, and venison was his favorite. Each day after court business was finished, the king and his hunting party would ride to the north of Varanasi and hunt deer. The king expected all the villagers to quit whatever they were doing, go into the woods, and chase the deer out into the open. This meant the farmers had to leave their fields, the millers had to leave their mills, the bakers had to leave their ovens, and so on. It was very inconvenient for the villagers who were trying to accomplish their daily tasks.

One day when everyone was heading out into the forest to chase the deer, a young girl had an idea. "Why don't we just herd all the deer to the king's fenced pleasure park on the edge of the city? Then the king can go there whenever he wishes, and we won't have to leave our duties every day," she said. Her idea spread among the villagers, who agreed that it was a very good plan.

The next day, well before the king's arrival, the villagers formed a three-mile ring of people around the area and began to drive the deer toward the king's pleasure park. It was a most successful drive, and both the Branch herd and the Banyan herd were caught in the effort. When the deer were all secured, the villagers sent word to the king, who rode with his hunting party to the park. The little girl who had the idea greeted the king, saying: "Your majesty, we have driven a great quantity of deer into your park so you will have a much easier time getting the meat for your table. We hope it pleases you." Indeed the king was pleased, and he complimented and rewarded the villagers for their enterprise.

As the king was viewing the great herd in the park he noticed two large, golden deer of great beauty moving among the herd. He declared that those two deer must always be spared, and could not be shot for his table. He then took his bow and arrow and rode into the herd and shot a doe. She was wounded by the first shot, and it took more arrows before she finally died.

As time went on the king stopped hunting in the park and just sent his cook to kill a deer for his table everyday. As might be expected, the daily hunt was a chaotic and terrifying occurrence for the deer. Many times deer were wounded without being killed, or injured in the tumultuous chase.

The Banyan king finally called all the deer together for a council. He said, "My friends, perhaps we must endure this daily horror, but we can insure that deer other than the victim do not become wounded or injured during the hunt. I propose that we draw lots to select the sacrifice for the king's table, rotating between the two herds." Both herds agreed this would eliminate unnecessary suffering and they adopted the idea.

The lottery system reduced injuries in both herds, but one day a pregnant doe from the Branch herd drew the sacrificial lot. The doe went to the Branch king and pleaded with him, "Oh great king, please allow me to delay my time for sacrifice until I give birth to my fawn. It only seems fair that he should have a chance at life even if I must forfeit mine."

The Branch king felt sympathy for the doe, but after some consideration said, "I am sorry. If I give you an exemption, then everyone who draws the sacrificial lot will come to me with a reason why he or she should also be spared."

Heartbroken by the thought of her unborn fawn perishing with her, the doe decided to approach the Banyan king, which she did, and explained again her plight.

The Banyan king felt a deep sense of compassion for the doe and her unborn fawn and said, "I understand. You go rest in the gardens and I will see that your turn is taken care of."

With that the Banyan king went to the place by the stream designated for the daily sacrifice, laid his head on the tree stump that served as the block, and waited. As was the custom, the king's cook arrived to dispatch that day's deer. Astonished to see the golden deer offering himself for sacrifice, he exclaimed, "The king has said that this deer is never to be harmed. What shall I do?" Deciding to put the matter before the king himself, the cook hurried back to the palace.

Equally astonished by this turn of events, the king rode to the garden. When he saw the great golden deer at the sacrificial block the king said, "King of the Deer, I have granted you your life. How is it that I now find you here?"

"Your majesty, I was approached by a fine doe, large with young, who had drawn today's lot. She begged to be spared so her fawn might live. I could not justly make another deer take her place, but I could take it myself, and so I have."

"Great deer," said the king, "I have not seen compassion this noble among humankind. What a treasured example and lesson this is for us all. You have demonstrated what it means to be a true leader and a creature of love. I will spare both your life and hers."

The Banyan deer rose from the block and said in a humble voice, "It is wonderful and generous of you that we two are spared, but what about the rest of the deer?"

"They are spared as well. I will eat meat no longer. You have shown me that animals can have virtues that surpass those of humans. I will kill no more," vowed the king.

Thus the Banyan and Branch herds were both released from the pleasure garden and returned to their normal feeding grounds.

THE TALKATIVE TORTOISE

Long ago on a beautiful lake in the foothills of the Himalaya Mountains there lived two young geese. They enjoyed the lovely lake, its surface dappled with water lily and lotus blossoms. Flowering trees filled with every kind of songbird grew along the lake's shore, and it was lined with gorgeous stone outcroppings. It was on one of these stones that the two geese first met the tortoise who was to become their close friend. He was a most peculiar tortoise in that he was extremely talkative. He was rarely silent, enjoying nothing more than conversing for hours with the geese. The geese seemed to overlook this character flaw in the tortoise, focusing on his kindness, generosity, and gentle nature.

The geese and the tortoise were inseparable all through the summer and fall. Then came the winter, the season for the geese to migrate to their winter feeding grounds. As the time drew near for them to go, all three friends were all quite sad, knowing the tortoise would have to be left behind.

"I would walk," said the tortoise, "but I'm sure by the time I got there it would be time for you to return here. And then I would . . ."

"Yes, yes," broke in the geese. "That would certainly not work."

They thought and thought about the situation and finally the geese had what they considered a workable idea.

"Good Tortoise," they said to their friend, "is it true that tortoises have such a strong bite that once they latch onto something nothing can make them let loose until they are ready?"

"It most certainly is," replied the tortoise. "We have jaws like iron traps. Why we are . . ."

"Well then," interrupted the geese, "this is our idea. We will find a strong stick and we will each hold one end in our bills. Then you can take hold of the stick in the center, grasping it firmly with your strong bite, and we will fly you to our winter feeding grounds. If it works, we will not have to be separated and we can spend the entire year together. There is just one thing you must remember. You cannot speak for the entire flight. If you speak you will lose your grip and fall."

"What a marvelous idea!" exclaimed the tortoise. "It is going to be wonderful to fly high above the ground and see all that goes on below. I am so excited . . ."

Later that day the geese had made all the necessary preparations, including securing a strong stick, and they were ready to go. They had the tortoise bite the stick firmly and off they went. The plan worked exactly as they had hoped. The two strong young geese had no problem lifting the tortoise—although they did have to fly somewhat lower than they were accustomed—and in no time they were on their way to the winter feeding grounds. As they were flying quite low over a village, the children all gathered to exclaim at the very unusual sight of the geese carrying the tortoise.

60

One child shouted up to the tortoise, "Fine Tortoise, that is the strangest thing we have ever seen. Why in the world are those two geese carrying you about?!"

Thrilled by the experience of flight, without thinking the tortoise opened his mouth and shouted, "These are my fine friends and they are taking me to their winter feeding grounds!"

In answering the children the tortoise had, of course, released his hold on the stick and he immediately fell to the ground.

His two friends were griefstricken and circled back to see if by chance he might have somehow survived the fall, but, as they expected, his shell had broken and he was dead.

The geese had no choice but to continue on their way.

With tears in his eyes one goose said to the other, "I should never have suggested such a plan. He would still be alive back in his lake."

"Do not blame yourself," said the second goose. "Our friend the tortoise knew very well what he had to do, but he could not keep his mouth closed. His downfall was his weakness for talking too much."

THE PARTRIDGE, THE MONKEY, AND THE ELEPHANT

Long ago in the foothills of the great Himalayan mountains there grew a giant banyan tree. It was the frequent meeting place for three friends: a partridge, a monkey, and an elephant. They had been friends ever since they could remember, but recently their friendship had been strained with increasingly frequent arguments and disagreements. The companions did not want this to continue and perhaps cause an end to their long-term friendship. They decided that they needed more structure in their relationship. To achieve this they would determine who was senior among them, and take that individual as their leader. The other two would then follow the senior's lead, since after all, that was the way of the world.

They decided to use the giant banyan tree as the standard to establish who was the eldest.

"How large was the banyan tree when you first remember it?" asked the partridge to the elephant.

The elephant thought long and hard and then said, "When I was a calf, I remember the banyan tree was but a seedling that would brush my stomach when I walked over the top of it."

The same question was put to the monkey who quickly responded, "My dear friends, I can recall that as an infant sitting on the ground, I would lean over to munch the top sprouts of the tiny scrub that was to become this banyan tree."

Finally the question came to the partridge. "My memory of this giant tree goes back even further," responded the bird with a fond tone in her voice, "I remember another giant banyan tree that grew on the other side of the river. I ate the fruit, which contained the seeds of that tree, and I then flew here and left the seeds in my droppings. The tree we now see behind us grew from those seeds."

Both the monkey and the elephant conceded that the partridge was most certainly the elder of the friends and she should have the position of honor. From then on they would be respectful to her and follow her counsel. The partridge took her new position earnestly. She decided that they all needed to treat each other with respect and dignity, thus ending the circumstances that led to their arguments and ensuring that their friendship would continue all their days.

THE RED MONKEY AND THE BLACK MONKEY

THE RED MONKEY AND THE BLACK MONKEY

ong ago there was a dense forest outside the great city of Varanasi. During the rainy season, showers often poured down on it for a week at a time. During one of those seemingly endless downpours an old black monkey, drenched to the skin, was wearily making his way through the forest seeking shelter from the rain. After hours of searching he came upon a cozy, rock-sheltered cave with a young red monkey sitting at its small entrance.

He thought to himself, "This young monkey will surely invite an elder to share his warm and cozy abode." He meekly stood in front of the cave and waited for an invitation to enter, but none came. The young monkey pretended not to even notice him.

This angered the old monkey and he thought, "If this little fellow will not invite me in, I will trick him out." He puffed up his belly as if he had just gorged himself and said, "My, those were the best ripe figs I have ever had, so juicy and sweet."

The red monkey showed a sudden interest in the old black monkey and said, "Hello Uncle, how are you? You speak of ripe figs. Are they far from here?"

"Not at all," said the black monkey. "I will give you directions and you will be there in no time at all." So off the red monkey went to find the figs and the black monkey went into the shelter and warmth of the cave.

Some time later the red monkey returned. He had searched and searched in the direction that the black monkey had sent him but found not a single fig. The rain had not let up for a minute and the red monkey was soaked and chilled. He found the black monkey sitting at the mouth of cave.

Realizing that the black monkey had tricked him, the red monkey thought he might try the same tactic. He rubbed his stomach and said, "I was happy to honor my elder by lending him my shelter, and what a fine bit of advice you gave me, Uncle. I have never had such fine figs. There are still plenty more waiting for you."

The old black monkey stayed where he was, stared unblinkingly at the young monkey, and said, "Were you honoring me when you ignored me standing in the rain? It would take a very dull monkey to fall for his own trick. Be off with you, and next time show better manners to your elders."

Humbled and thoroughly drenched, the red monkey went off to seek shelter elsewhere.

THE THREE FISH

**L**ong ago in the foothills of the Great Himalayan Mountains, three fish swam in the wild upper reaches of the Ganges River. The first fish was called Over-Thoughtful, as he pondered all questions for so long that he never came up with answers and could not take action on his own. The second fish was called Thoughtless, as he did not think at all but simply charged ahead on his first impulse. The third fish was called Thoughtful, as he considered his circumstances carefully and made his judgments wisely.

The three fish were swimming downstream, feeding as they went. The food supply kept getting better and better the farther they swam, but Thoughtful knew that men who netted and trapped fish lived downstream, and he said to the two others, "We should turn around and swim back upstream now so we don't get caught by the humans and end up as someone's supper."

Thoughtless just knew that the food supply was getting better and better and he simply charged ahead, feeding as he went. Over-Thoughtful could not make up his mind, so he simply followed Thoughtless further downstream. Thoughtful, against his better judgment but worried about his two friends, followed some distance behind.

Sure enough, further downstream Thoughtless and Over-Thoughtful blindly rushed into a fisherman's net. Thoughtful from his careful distance saw what happened and said to himself, "The two fools will end up on someone's plate if I don't act now." With great speed he swam to the front of the net and splashed as if a fish had broken through and gone upstream, then he quickly swam around and splashed at the other end of the net and made it appear as if a fish had broken through the net and was swimming downstream. The fishermen seeing all this action felt that their net must have developed holes and pulled it in by one corner, allowing Thoughtless and Over-Thoughtful to escape.

The two hapless fish were both so frightened that they finally saw the wisdom of Thoughtful's advice and swam back upstream with him to the wild country where, even if feeding was sparser, they were safe from the nets of men.

THE THREE FISH

THE WEAK-WILLED WOLF

THE WEAK-WILLED WOLF

ong ago on the banks of the great Ganges river there lived a wolf who made his home on a high, rocky outcropping along the river. One night the winter floods began as the wolf slept, and when he awoke he found to his surprise that he was now on an island in the middle of the river with dangerous currents whirling swiftly all around him.

He was stranded without any food. He said to himself, "Well, there must be some good side to this situation. I have no food and absolutely nothing to do with my time. I know!" he said with excitement in his voice, "I will partake of a holy fast. I have always been a greedy wolf who has only been interested in satisfying my own wants. I now have the time and circumstances to fast, meditate, and contemplate how I can become a better and more holy wolf. I pledge I shall not eat until the river goes down."

With that pledge the wolf assumed the lotus position that he had seen holy men take, and he looked very serious about the commitment he had made. Just then, to his astonishment, a plump little goat washed up on his rocky little island.

The wolf took one look at the little goat and said, "I will start my fast tomorrow," and he leapt at the little goat. But the goat was incredibly quick, and each time the wolf charged at him, he nimbly and easily avoided the wolf's attack. The wolf charged the goat time and time again, but he never even came close to capturing the agile little creature. Finally, completely exhausted, he gave up the attempt and went back to his meditation seat. When he had caught his breath he said, "Well, I did not break my fast and I shall now continue with my holy ways."

A great white pelican had been swimming not far from the island and observed the wolf's conversion, relapse, and re-conversion. Unable to endure the hypocrisy, she swam near the island and said, "Mr. Wolf, you are a most remarkable creature. You make a vow, break the vow, and then act as if the vow was never broken. Vows are always as difficult to keep as they are easy to make. A holy wolf indeed!"

THE TWIN DEER

THE TWIN DEER

ong ago there was a wise elder deer in one of the large deer herds that used to roam to the north of the great Indian city of Varanasi. Many of the females of the herd would bring their sons to the elder deer to learn the ways of the forest and of survival. One day the elder's youngest sister brought her twin sons to the great teacher and said, "Dear brother, my sons are now of the age at which they need to better understand the ways of the forest and how to survive in these difficult times. Would you please give them lessons?"

"I would be most happy to do so, my sister. Have them both come to me tomorrow when the sun is at midday," replied the elder brother.

At midday of the following day one of the twins arrived for his lesson, but the other did not. The missing twin had a reputation for being foolish, and he had decided he would rather play in the forest than listen to what some old deer had to say. The elder deer gave the attentive twin his lesson and set a time for the next day. This went on for weeks, with the foolish twin skipping every lesson.

One day when the foolish twin was out frolicking in the forest, he stumbled directly into a hunter's snare. He panicked and tore and ripped at the snare only to have it tighten so much that his leg was deeply cut and bleeding. He fought and panicked until he was covered with sweat and shaking with fear. Finally the hunter came to check his snare and found the trembling young deer in his trap. He slew the deer and took its meat back to his village. News of the tragedy soon made its way back to the deer herd and the twins' mother was heartbroken. The uncle was also deeply saddened.

The wise twin continued his lessons with his uncle until the uncle felt he had learned all he needed to know. As luck would have it, some days later when the wise twin was out with some of the herd he too was caught in a hunter's snare. He gave the cry of alarm and all the rest of the herd escaped into the forest. When the rest of the herd learned of the second twin's capture, the mother was beyond herself in grief. Her brother came to her and told her that she would soon see her son again, because he had been a very good student.

The wise twin's reaction to his capture was very different than his brother's. First, he used his hoofs and dug up the ground all around the snare area to make it look as if he had been struggling. Next he lay on his side and took air into himself to make it look as if he were bloated. Then he opened his eyes widely and rolled his eyes back in his head and let his tongue hang out of the side of his mouth. He gave no motion at all of breath. When he had accomplished all these preparations he looked so dead that the blue-bottle flies were buzzing around him and crows were gathering.

The hunter returned to check his snares and saw the deer lying there in such a state. "My," he thought to himself, "This deer must have been caught early in the morning. He has been dead for some time and is already going bad. I had better butcher him now."

The hunter removed the snare from the deer's leg and turned to his pack to get his knives. At that instant the young deer sprang to life and in a cloud of dust was out of sight in a flash. The hunter stood in the dust, stunned. The deer had certainly outwitted him.

When the wise twin returned to the herd, his mother wept tears of joy. His teacher was also there to greet him, but he was not surprised to see his pupil return. The young stag was reaping the benefits of being a good student.

THE WICKED CRANE

Long ago in a wetland area of northeastern India there was a small pond that was well populated with a variety of fish. Every year during the dry season the pond's water got very low, and sometimes the fish were in danger. A crane was observing the pond and trying to figure out how he could eat as many fish as possible.

He was standing by the edge of the pond contemplating the problem when the leader of the fish noticed him standing there but, unlike an ordinary crane, not attempting to catch any fish. The fish surfaced and said, "Mr. Crane, what are you thinking about as you stand by our pond without attempting to catch us?"

"Well," said the crane, "I was thinking about you fish and your welfare."

"That is most unlikely," replied the fish. "There has never been a crane who gave a care about fish other than to eat us."

"Not so," said the deceitful crane. "This pond is most certainly going to dry up during the drought and you will all perish. It would be sad to see such a thing. I know of a large, deep beautiful pond not far from here, and I would be happy to transport you, one by one, to that new home."

"You will most certainly eat us, one by one, if we consent to such a plan," said the fish.

"If you don't believe me let me take one of you there and bring him back with his own report of the pond," suggested the crane.

The fish held a meeting and a big, tough, one-eyed fish volunteered to make the trip. The crane carefully took him in his mouth and carried him to the large pond. It was just as the crane has described—spacious, deep, full of food, and very beautiful. The crane then returned the one-eyed fish to the small pond, where he gave a splendid report of the pond the crane had shown him, and the fish all agreed that since as they would not have to worry every dry season it would be a much better home.

When the transport began the crane took the one-eyed fish first, but this time he flew over the pond and landed in a large tree by the shore. He plunged the fish into the fork of the tree and ate him, letting his bones drop down to the base of the tree. The crane returned to the small pond and kindly took each fish, one by one, gently into his mouth, flew them to the tree, and ate them all.

After eating all the fish in the small pond, the crane noticed that a large crab remained there. He approached the crab and said, "Mr. Crab, I have taken all the fish from this pond to a fine new home. Wouldn't you like to join them? You will be quite lonely here all by yourself." The crab looked at the bloated crane and knew that he had not taken any fish to a new home, but the crab thought the crane needed to be taught a lesson.

"Lord Crane, how would you take me to this new home?" said the crab.

"I would carefully take you in my mouth, Mr. Crab," replied the crane.

"My shell is hard and slippery. I'm afraid that you might accidentally drop me on the way. I will go with you if let me hold onto your neck with my great claw, for I have a very good grip," said the crab.

The crane was too full of himself, and all the fish he had just eaten, to think that he, the trickster, could ever be tricked, so he said the arrangement would be fine. The crab got a firm grip on the crane's neck and off they went. They went flying over the large pond and the crab innocently said to the crane, "Uncle, isn't that the pond to which you took all the other fish?"

The crane replied in a taunting voice as he landed in his eating tree, "Well, nephew, if you'll look below us at the pile of bones at the base of this tree you will see all your former neighbors from the small pond. Your shell will soon be on top of that pile."

Tightening his grip on the crane's neck the crab said, "I don't think so, you wicked crane. You will take me down to that pond immediately."

The crane's mouth was open and his eyes were bulging out and tearing. "All right, Lord Crab, no tighter please. I will take you down at once."

As they touched down on the mud at the edge of the pond the crab knew that the cruel crane would attack him as soon as he released his neck. The crab also thought of the fate of all the poor, trusting fish from the pond, and as the crane bent over to put the crab in the mud, the crab made one sharp clamp of his pincher and snipped the crane's head from his long neck as cleanly as a knife cutting a lotus stalk.

THE WICKED CRANE

THE WISE PARTRIDGE

THE WISE PARTRIDGE

Long ago in northeastern India near the Himalaya Mountains there lived a fine, strong young partridge. She enjoyed her days feeding on seeds and socializing with members of her flock, and she was known for her good sense and prudent ways. But one day she was not so prudent, and she failed to observe a fowler who was stalking her flock as they were feeding on grass seeds in a meadow. Only when it was too late did she see the net fly over their heads and drop down on at least half the flock.

As the partridge struggled to get free, the hunter carefully gathered up the net, making sure that none of the birds escaped. Then, one by one, he took the partridges out of the net and put them into a wooden cage. When the hunter took the wise partridge out of the net to transfer her to the trap she struggled and tried her best to escape, but without success.

The fowler knew he could take the birds to the market in town and sell them to the villagers for their dinner. But he also knew that if he fattened them up beyond their lean natural state he could get a considerably higher price for the birds. So he took them back to his home and fed the birds on grain and water. The birds were in a panic in the confines of the small cage and they wept and hopped about chaotically bumping into one another. But when the hunter came to feed them they eagerly ate and ate—that is, all except the wise partridge. She knew what was happening and decided not to eat so that she would grow thinner rather than fatter, becoming less desirable for a dinner table. It was difficult not to eat when the rich grain was offered to her, but she knew that her hunger pangs and increasingly gaunt appearance might be her only chance for survival.

When the hunter decided that the partridges were fat enough and was about to take them to market, he noticed that one bird was very thin. He reached in the cage and grasped her in his hand. He could feel her ribs distinctly under her feathers. He thought this quite strange and took the quail out the cage and laid her in his outstretched hand to see if he could discover why she was so gaunt. The wise partridge laid perfectly still until a moment when the hunter relaxed his grip; then, with all her remaining strength, she burst out of his hand and flew up into the sky. Thus she gained her freedom through her sacrifice. By not eating and bearing the pain of hunger she regained her life and the opportunity to eat her fill for years to come. She returned to what remained of her flock in the forest, told them her story of capture and escape, and they all vowed to keep a much more diligent lookout for hunters in the future.

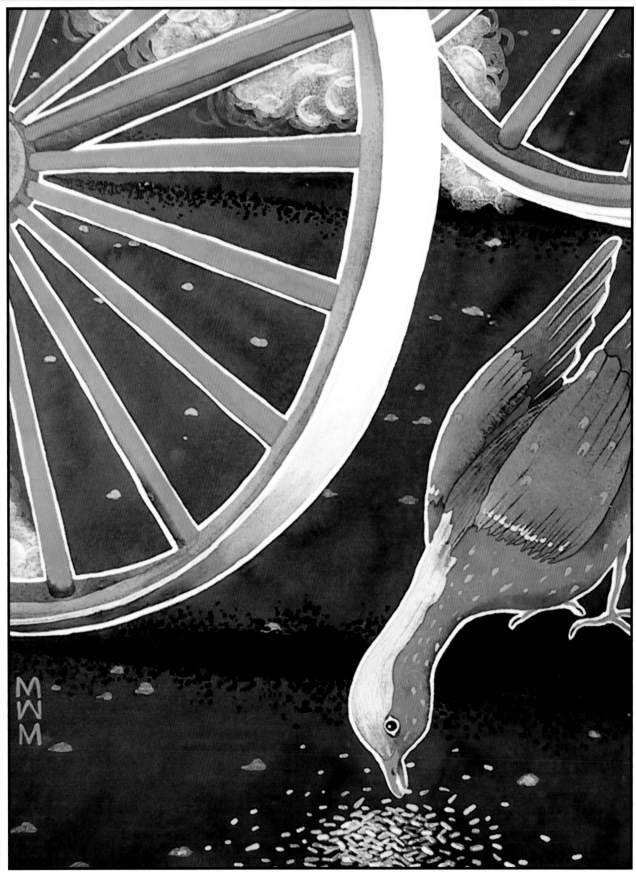

THE DOVE WITH A DOUBLE STANDARD

THE DOVE WITH A DOUBLE STANDARD

**L**ong ago there was an area of northeastern India inhabited by a large dove population. Most of the doves found their food on the forest floor, where they scratched and pecked for seeds among the fallen leaves and branches. There was also a wide road running through the forest, and many wagons passed along it carrying loads of grains and beans to be taken to the great markets in Varanasi. As the wagons bumped along, some of the grain and beans inevitably spilled on the road. Sleek carriages of the noblemen pulled by speedy horses were also common on the road.

There was one very outgoing dove who secretly frequented the great road and ate the spilled delicacies that the wagons left, but she told all the other doves that they should never come to the road. She said, "Dear friends, the road is much too dangerous for birds. It abounds with perils—elephants, fierce oxen, rushing horses, and many other menaces wait to trample feeding birds in their way." She told the birds this so often that she became known as "Warner." But she was greedy for the easy food near the road and often went there clandestinely herself.

One day she was feeding on some particularly delicious rice and saw a carriage approaching. She said to herself, "That horse is not coming all that fast. I'm sure I can eat a few more seeds before I need to fly." But she had misjudged. The horse came rushing like the wind, and the next time Warner looked up the carriage was on her. The wheel crushed her body and she was instantly killed.

After some time had passed, her companions wondered where she had gone and began looking for her. One dove flying over the road spied the lifeless remains of Warner lying on the roadside beside a small pile of spilled rice. The dove could not believe his eyes. After all the times she had warned everyone to stay away from the road, there she was crushed on the thoroughfare. He flew back to the flock and they all flew to the road and perched in a large tree above the shattered body of Warner. One of the flock said, "Her advice was good. It is shame she did not take it herself. Greed can lead to the saddest of results."

80

THE ANIMALS AND THE HERMIT

Long ago a holy man wishing to develop a deeper understanding of life came to live as a hermit in a remote area of the Himalayan foothills. One summer a parching drought went on month after month. As all the streams had dried up in the sweltering sun, the hermit dug a well to provide himself with water.

The animals of the area began suffering deeply from the lack of water and many were on the verge of perishing. The hermit felt a deep compassion for the animals and decided to help them. He cut down a large dead tree and hollowed out the center to make a large drinking trough. It was very difficult work in the extreme heat of the drought but, knowing the animals would not survive much longer, he persisted. When he had finished the trough, he began filling it with buckets from his well. Once again, it was strenuous work, but he accomplished it.

The animals of the forest could smell the water they so desperately craved and slowly began to come to the trough to drink. First the birds, rabbits, and squirrels came. Then the deer and wild boar arrived to drink. And finally even the great tiger came in the spirit of peace and drank from the hermit's trough.

The hermit had to work almost continuously to keep the trough full of water for the steady stream of thirsty animals. His labor was so time-consuming that he neglected to forage for the roots and fruits that made up his diet. The animals could see that he was growing weak, and they decided to return his kindness. They knew the places deep in the woods where edible roots, berries, and even some fruits still remained, and they went out and gathered some for the hermit. When they returned with the food the hermit was deeply moved by this display of their gratitude. During the drought the hermit kept filling the trough for the animals and the animals kept bringing him food. When the drought finally ended and the rains came, the streams filled once again. The hermit no longer needed to fill the trough and he could now gather his own food. But his close relationship to the animals did not end. The animals often came and rested by his hut or perched in nearby trees, happy to be with the friend who had saved their lives.

THE CROW AND THE RUDDY DUCKS

Long ago in the great city of Varanasi there lived a crow who made his living as a scavenger, eating the corpses of the dead and stealing food left by people on their window ledges. He was a wily bird and never satisfied with what he had. One day he decided that he would like to change his menu and flew out along the Ganges River to see if any dead fish were lying along the shore. As he was searching he noticed two beautiful ruddy ducks swimming in the river. He thought to himself, "What a gorgeous red color these ducks are. I wonder what they eat to be such a glorious hue? I shall find out and eat it myself to change my color from this dingy gray and black to that rich earthen red."

He flew down and landed on the bank near the ducks and said, "My dear feathered friends, may I ask what kind of fish or meat you eat that gives your feathers such a wonderful color?"

The ducks looked at the crow with a skeptical eye knowing the reputation of such birds. "Mr. Crow," replied the male duck, "We eat no fish or meat of any kind. To eat the flesh of another being would go against our very nature. We wish only peace and happiness for all. We eat only weeds from the bottom of the river. That is adequate nourishment for us."

"Surely," said the crow, "weeds could not create the beautiful color of your feathers. There must be some other food you are eating and not telling me. I eat a vast variety of meats and whatever else I can find and I have only these drab hues to ornament my body."

"Crow," said the female duck, "we eat only weeds. Beauty is not created only by what you eat but also by what you do. You are a creature who steals and eats the flesh of your fellow beings. You cannot expect to have beauty. Change your ways. Live for the well being of others and beauty will be yours."

The crow gave the ducks a disdainful look and said, "If that's the case, I don't want your good looks. I prefer my own ways." And with a shrill cry of "Caw! Caw! Caw!" he flew off to continue his search for dead fish.

THE CROW AND THE RUDDY DUCKS

THE RURU DEER

THE RURU DEER

Long ago in a kingdom of northeast India there lived a remarkable creature called a ruru deer. He lived in the deepest forest of the kingdom in order to hide himself from human eyes. He was the most beautiful creature of the entire forest. His coat glistened as if it were pure gold and was dappled with dazzling spots of color that looked like rubies, sapphires, and emeralds. His large, bright, blue eyes expressed warmth and kindness. His beautiful horns and hoofs looked as if they were polished marble. The ruru deer knew that his beauty would make him irresistible to the greed of men. He had learned all the tricks of men, with their snares and traps and nets. In his kindness he also taught the other creatures of the forest how to avoid mankind's evil ploys.

One day, after a strong rain, as he made his way through the forest, the ruru deer heard some strange sounds coming from the river. He quickly made his way to the riverbank and saw a man being swept along by the swollen current. The man was screaming for help, "Please, oh please, someone help me! I am about to go under!"

The deer was touched by the man's plight. He leapt into the water and swam against the raging current to the drowning man. "Get on my back," he calmly said to the man, "and I will take you the safety."

The amazed man managed to pull himself on the spectacular creature's back and the deer deftly swam to the river's edge. He took the exhausted man to a dry place and warmed him with the warmth of his own body. After the man rested and recuperated, the deer showed the man the way to return to the city. The man was deeply touched by the great kindness of the deer and said, "No one could have done me a greater service than you have. You have saved my life and shown me such benevolence. Is there anything I can do to repay you?"

"Gratitude," said the deer, "is a quality that should come naturally, but today it is called a great virtue. I am glad to see it in you. There is one thing you can do for me. You cannot relate a word to anyone about my existence. If humans hear that such a creature lives in these woods they will not rest until they have captured me."

"If you wish it, I will certainly keep your existence a secret. It is a very small price for what you have done for me," said the man.

In the city there lived a queen who had dreams that often became reality. One night she dreamed of the ruru deer. She saw it in all its glory, with its jewel-dappled golden hue. In her dream the great deer was standing in the throne room of the palace with the king and all his court was listening to its teaching. She awoke in a state of blissful excitement. She went immediately to the king and told him of her wonderful dream. The king knew that the queen's dreams were very often true and he sent out his huntsmen to seek the deer. He also issued a proclamation describing the deer and stating that anyone who helped to find it would be given a fine home and a large reward.

The man who had been saved by the ruru deer lived in the city and heard the proclamation over and over again. He was a poor man and the temptation of wealth was very difficult for him to resist. He knew that he should not betray the deer, but he also knew that he could help his family in many ways with the reward. He struggled with his decision but finally decided to go the king and tell what he knew.

The king was very excited by the news and asked the man to immediately take him to the area of the forest where the deer lived. They departed with a large troop of the king's soldiers and descended on the forest of the ruru deer. The army formed a circle around the area, slowly drawing it tighter and tighter. The king and his guide made their way into a dark thicket, and there was the ruru deer. The light struck him from above and he glowed like magic. The deer knew he was surrounded and could not escape. The king drew an arrow and placed it in his bow. As he was to let the arrow fly the deer said, "Your Majesty, please delay your arrow and first tell me how you came to find me here."

The amazed king put down his bow and said that the man behind him, his guide, had brought him to this place. The deer immediately recognized the man as the one he had saved from the river and said, "An ungrateful man is better left in the river."

The king was perplexed by this statement and asked the deer to explain. The deer told the king the story of how he had rescued the guide, who hung his head in shame. At the conclusion of the story the king turned to the man and asked, "Is this true?" Without lifting his head the man said, "Yes." The king lifted his bow and pointed it at the man and said, "There is only one punishment that would fit such deceit." And he prepared to loose the arrow. The ruru deer then stepped between the man and the king, "Please don't wound one who is already wounded. His greed has wounded him as it has wounded so many men. Men are attracted to wealth as moths are attracted to the flame. Please let him live to learn from his mistakes," said the deer.

The king was overwhelmed by the mercy the deer felt toward a person who had already returned his kindness with such contempt. "I will grant him his life," said the king, "and I will also grant you yours. You shall always be safe anywhere in my kingdom."

"I accept your generosity great king. In return is there anything I can do for you?" asked the deer.

Yes," said the king, "if you would be so kind as to return to the court with me and teach my people about mercy as you have shown me today. It would be a great benefit to my people."

And so the deer did travel to the court, and he taught in the throne room, thus fulfilling the queen's dream.

THE SENSITIVE OX

ong ago in northwest India in the land of Gandhara there lived a kind farmer. One year he purchased a bull ox calf, to which he became very attached. He raised the calf with great kindness and care, treating it as if it were one of his sons. The farmer was so pleased with the ox that he gave him the name of True Happiness.

When the ox grew to his full size he was a magnificent creature, massive in musculature and possessing great strength. Wishing to repay the kindness that his owner had shown him, one day the ox suggested, "Good master, with my strength I know I can pull more weight than any other ox in this region. Why don't you find a wealthy merchant willing to wager one thousand pieces of silver that I can move one hundred fully laden carts."

"My wonderful True Happiness," said the farmer, "you propose quite a wager. Are sure you can pull that much weight?"

"That much and more," replied True Happiness.

So off to town went the farmer. He made inquiries to find the merchant with the strongest oxen in town, paid him a visit, and after some casual conversation made the claim that he had an ox that could move one hundred fully laden carts.

"No!" said the merchant. "There is no ox in the world that could move such a weight."

"There is at my farm," said the farmer.

"Then make a bet on it," said the merchant.

"I will wager one thousand pieces of silver that my ox can move one hundred fully laden carts," said the farmer.

"Done!" said the merchant.

In two days' time all the arrangements were made. The carts were loaded and tied together at the edge of town. True Happiness had been bathed and fed scented rice. A garland of flowers had been hung around his neck, and he was yoked to the long procession of carts. The farmer looked back at the huge weight the ox was going to try to pull and became very worried about his one thousand pieces of silver. He took his seat on the first cart and shouted at True Happiness, "Go on, you brute! Move the carts, you wretch! Pull with all your might, you devil!"

True Happiness could not believe his ears, "Devil! Wretch! Brute!" He had never been called such names in his life. The ox considered himself none of those things and his legs became like posts as he stood his ground, not moving an inch even when the farmer used his whip and heaped further abuse on him.

It was obvious that the farmer had lost the wager and he paid up and went back to his farm, where he fell on his bed overwhelmed with grief at his loss. True Happiness found his way to the farmhouse and stuck his head in the open window. "Good master," the ox said, "are you sleeping?"

THE SENSITIVE OX

"Sleeping?" said the farmer. "How could I sleep after losing one thousand pieces of silver? How could you do that to me? You did not even try to move those carts!"

"Master," said True Happiness, "in all the years I lived with you, have I ever been a trouble to you? Have I ever hurt anyone? Have I ever shown any wickedness to you or your family?"

"Not once," said the farmer.

"Then why," the ox questioned, "did you call me a wretch and a brute and a devil? And why did you strike me with a whip? You have never done so before."

The farmer was silent for a moment and felt somewhat shamed, "True Happiness, I understand clearly now. In my greed for money and fear of the loss of it, I forgot what a dear friend you are to me. I am sorry."

The ox said, "Go to the merchant and offer to wager two thousand pieces of silver on the same conditions. I think he will gladly take the bet."

The farmer did so and the merchant jumped at the chance of what seemed an easy victory. The carts were reset and all was ready. When the farmer brought True Happiness into town the people along the way laughed and jeered at the ox who had not moved the carts an inch the last time.

True Happiness was yoked to the carts and the farmer took his seat, this time with no whip. When all was ready the farmer said in a kind voice, "True Happiness, my wonderful ox, my fine friend, move the last cart to where the first is now." With intense effort and bulging muscles, the ox began striding and the line of carts followed along until the last cart stood where the first one had been. The farmer collected his two thousand pieces of silver and the amazed crowd cheered and cheered.

True Happiness turned to the crowd and said, "Kind and gentle words can move heavy loads. Insults and cruel words move nothing but hurt feelings."

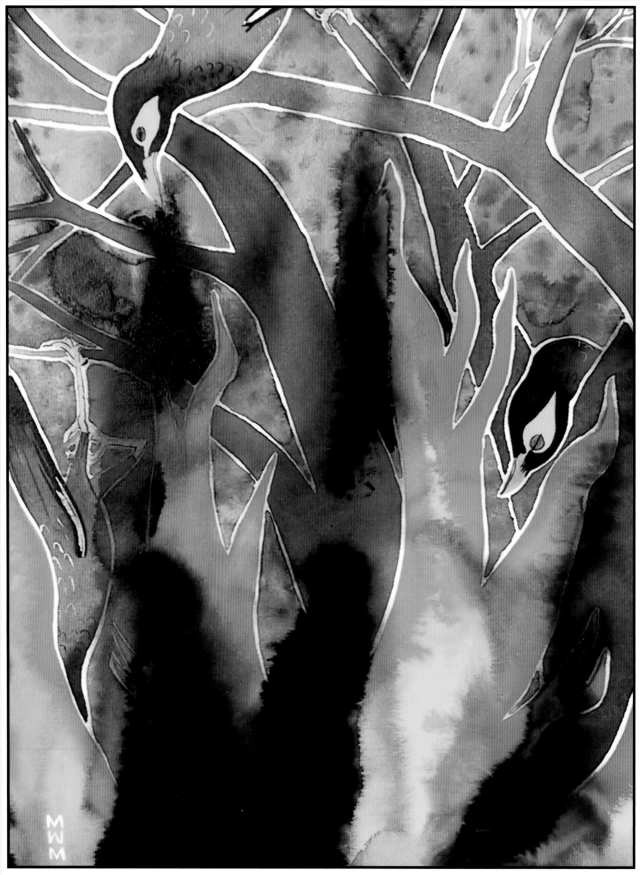

The Myna Birds and the Burning Tree

ong ago in the lush forest south of the great city of Varanasi a flock of myna birds roosted in a large old *pippala* tree. They and their ancestors had been roosting in this same tree for decades. One windy day the wise leader of the flock noticed that two dead branches were rubbing against one another is such a way that smoke was being generated by the friction. It was the dry season. Parched leaves and dead wood filled the old tree. He thought to himself, "If fire breaks out it will rapidly spread through these old leaves and dry wood. The flock is in real danger."

He quickly flew throughout the tree with the warning, "We must fly from this tree at once. It could burst into flames at any moment!" The birds with good common sense followed his advice immediately and flew out of the tree to neighboring trees several hundred yards away.

But there were skeptics. Some said, "Oh, he is such a worrier. He sees crocodiles in drops of dew." Others laughed in agreement, saying they had never seen a tree burst into flames. But as they were jeering at their leader the tree did just that. The flames broke out rapidly at the friction point and spread with amazing speed. The wind sent thick smoke into the upper braches. The birds who had not flown away were immediately overcome by the smoke and dropped into the flames below.

From a safe distance the wise birds watched with horror as their friends perished from their foolish ignorance.

THE OXEN AND THE PIG

**L**ong ago on a prosperous farm in the outskirts of Rajgir there lived two brother oxen. The elder was called Big Red and the younger Little Red. The farmer had a large family and his eldest daughter was soon to wed. The oxen worked all day long in the fields or pulled heavily laden carts. At the end of the day they were fed grass hay and grain chaff. One evening they were eating their simple meal and Little Red looked over to the comfortable sty where a pig, called Lotus Root, was enjoying a large meal of sweetened rice porridge and delicious looking table scraps. Little Red lamented, "Dear brother, why is that we, who labor all day long for the farmer, receive only hay and chaff for our dinner, while this pig does absolutely nothing all day and receives cooked porridge and all types of wonderful food?"

Big Red replied, "My beloved little brother, do not be envious of Lotus Root's fine food. She will pay dearly for the enjoyment she is now having. Soon one of the farmer's daughters will be wed and Lotus Root will be slaughtered and cut up into little bits for the wedding curry. Our honest labor assures us simple food and a long life."

Soon the wedding day came and everything that Big Red had prophesied came to be. When the knife was taken to Lotus Root, Little Red shuddered at the terrible shrieks and said to his brother, "Oh wise brother, our food is a hundred, no, a thousand times better than the fancy fare of poor Lotus Root."

THE OXEN AND THE PIG

The Lion and the Boar

THE LION AND THE BOAR

Long ago in the foothills of the great Himalayas there lived a mighty lion who made his home in a cozy cave. One day the lion killed a large water buffalo and feasted until he was stuffed. On his way back to his cave for a nap he decided to stop at a lake to quench his thirst. As he approached the lake he saw a boar who was drinking. He was far too full to think of eating the boar, but hoping it might come back another day when he was hungry again, he did not want to frighten it away from the lake, so he slunk back into the brush. The boar saw the retreating lion, and in his vanity thought the beast was slinking away out of fear. The boar said to himself, "Due to my strength and fearsome appearance this lion flees my presence. This day I will fight this cowardly lion!"

The boar called to the lion, "Lion, come back here and fight like a warrior. I fear you not."

The lion was very surprised to here such arrogance coming from the wild pig, but he decided to use it for his advantage. He said to the boar, "My friend, I'm sorry I cannot fight you today, but I would be happy to meet your challenge one week from today at this very spot."

The boar was delighted and accepted the conditions. He went back to his herd and told them of his adventure. He said, "I will conquer this lion and make the name of all boars famous forever!"

The leader of the herd said, "You must be mad! There is no boar who can kill a lion. You are going to die."

This made the boar think and reconsider his ill-conceived arrogance. "Well then, what am I going to do? If I do not go he will surely hunt me down," lamented the boar. "Yes," said the leader, "and in doing so he will find the rest of us and many will die. You must go to the challenge. But I have an idea. For each of the next six days you must go to the dunghill and roll in feces, letting it dry each day and coat your body. On the seventh day, just before the fight, moisten yourself with dew-drops to activate the foulest smell possible. Go to the designated spot for the fight early, and position yourself so that the wind is at your back."

The boar followed the leader's instructions to the letter. On the day of his fight with the lion, he stood by the lake encased in excrement and reeking foully. The lion, a fastidiously clean creature, was disgusted by the thick coating of feces on the boar. The stench was so powerful it made his eyes water. He said to the boar "I could not touch you much less bite you. You have won this fight, but with the most disgusting tactics I have ever encountered." And the lion went off to find his dinner in a less objectionable package.

The foolish boar was exhilarated. His inflated ego again puffed up and he rushed back to the herd to tell them of his great victory.

THE ANTELOPE, THE WOODPECKER, AND THE TORTOISE

THE ANTELOPE, THE WOODPECKER, AND THE TORTOISE

ong ago deep in the forest north of the great city of Varanasi three close friends lived by the shore of a clear, beautiful lake. The three friends were an antelope, a woodpecker, and a tortoise. They were as different in form as three creatures could be, but over time they had developed a deep love and respect for one another.

One day a hunter discovered the antelope's hoof prints down at the water's edge and carefully set a leather snare in hopes of catching him. That evening the antelope went down to the lake for his usual drink. In the dim, shadowy light of dusk he did not see the cleverly hidden snare and stepped directly into it. Immediately the leather straps tightened around his leg, and he was caught. In his fright he let out a loud cry for help.

The woodpecker and tortoise recognized the voice of their dear friend and with all speed made their way to the lake's edge. When they reached the distressed antelope and saw his dilemma they knew it would be the end of their friend if the hunter found him in the snare.

They thought for a while about what they could do and then the woodpecker said to the tortoise, "Do you think you could gnaw through those leather straps?"

"Well, yes, I could," said the tortoise, "but they are very thick and it will take me a long time to do so."

"You begin gnawing," said the woodpecker, "and I will see if I can delay the hunter."

The woodpecker flew to the hunter's hut and waited. In the morning the hunter rose, ate his breakfast, collected his hunting bag, and prepared to depart and check the snares he had set the previous day. As he opened his front door the woodpecker flew directly into his face. The hunter was frightened and shocked. "What a strange event, to have such a bird fly into one's face," he said, quite shaken. "I think I will take a rest before going out." With that he went back into his hut. After some hours he felt composed enough to try again, but this time he decided to leave from the back door instead. When he opened the door, the woodpecker was waiting and once again flew directly into his face. The stunned hunter said, "This is too much! Some bad luck will befall me today if I go out. I am simply going to stay in and rest."

The next morning he got up determined to check his snares; the woodpecker knew he could not stop him a second day. He flew back to the antelope and tortoise and said, "The hunter is coming now! I can forestall him no longer!"

The tortoise almost had the last strap chewed through. His mouth was sore and bleeding, but with much effort he bit through the last strap and the antelope bounded away just as the hunter arrived.

The woodpecker flew up to a high branch, but the exhausted tortoise could only lie on the ground, gasping for air. The hunter was amazed at the tortoise's rescue of the antelope and said, "Never have I seen such a thing! I may have lost the antelope, but at least I will have tortoise soup." He scooped up the tortoise and put him in his hunting sack.

The antelope observed the tortoise's capture from the brush and knew it was now his turn to do something to help his friend. He came out of the brush in full view of the hunter and pretended that the leg he had caught in the snare was very lame. He limped and made a show of walking very slowly. Seeing this, the hunter thought he might be able to catch the antelope; he quickly hung the bag with the tortoise on a low tree limb and ran after the antelope. The antelope led the hunter deep into the woods, staying just out of reach. When they were far enough from the lake, he quickly lost the hunter and made his way back to the tortoise.

With his long horns the antelope took the bag down from the tree and gently laid it on the ground. He slit the bag open with the sharp tip of his horn and released the tortoise from his captivity.

The antelope then said to the woodpecker and the tortoise, "You are the finest of friends. I owe my life to you, but I think we must take our families and migrate to a new place. If we stay here we will always be at risk from this hunter. I hope we will all meet again and I can be of service to you." The three friends then went to find new homes far away from the hunter and his threatening ways.

THE MONKEY KING

Long ago in fertile valleys of the foothills of the great Himalayan Mountains there grew a very special tree called a *peepul* tree. It was magnificent in its scale and beauty. When it blossomed in the spring, it seemed as if a huge white cloud was suspended in the forest; when its fruit ripened, it was delicious and fragrant beyond imagination.

This remarkable tree was home to a large troop of monkeys led by a wise and compassionate king—a very large, strong monkey, well loved by the entire troop. He was always willing to help even the smallest member of the group.

The monkeys lived on the fruit of the tree, and the king knew well how special its fruit was. One branch of the tree grew out over the Ganges River. The king was aware that if any fruit were to fall into the river, float downstream, and be discovered by men, their greed would not let them rest until they found the fruit's source, which would mean the end of the monkeys' happy home. Accordingly, each spring the king instructed the monkeys to pluck all of the blossoms off of the branches that overhung the river, and each spring they diligently did so—until one year they overlooked a single blossom that was concealed by leaves. The leaves also concealed the fruit as it grew, and when it ripened it fell into the river and was carried downstream. As fate would have it, the fruit made its way to the great city of Varanasi and became lodged in a fence in the river that confined a bathing area for the king and his wives.

The smell of the wonderful fruit was so strong and delightful that one of king's wives quickly found it and brought the never-seen-before fruit to the king. He had it analyzed by his wisest advisers, and finally they sliced it and ate the pieces. They were overwhelmed with the richest, sweetest flavor they had ever experienced. The king immediately decided he must find the source of the fruit.

The next day he set off along the river with a large troop of soldiers. They searched persistently day after day until finally, in the distance, they spotted the top of what seemed to be a very unusual tree. It was bold and rich in its color and had a massive structure. As they came closer they began to smell the fragrance of the fruit, and they knew their search was at an end.

As they approached the tree the king could see that its branches were full of monkeys eating the fruit he so desired. This infuriated him and he ordered his archers to destroy the monkeys. They encircled the tree and readied themselves to shoot the monkeys. With the soldiers surrounding the base of the tree, the monkeys could not run down to the ground, and there were no other trees close enough for them to jump to; there seemed to be no escape. As the archers began shooting, the monkeys panicked.

The monkey king thought hard about what he could do to help his followers. There was a tree on the other side of the river that the strongest monkeys might nearly reach, but the smaller ones most certainly could not jump the distance. The monkey king firmly gripped a flexible branch of the *peepul* tree with one foot and made a huge leap to the tree on the other side of the river. He barely made it, but he succeeded in keeping hold of the *peepul* branch with his foot and just barely grasping a limb of the tree on the other side with his hand—making his body into a bridge from one tree to the other.

He ordered the monkeys to hurry across to safety, and in their terror the entire troop bounded roughly across, stretching and bruising the monkey king in the process. When the last monkey had made its way across, the injured and exhausted monkey king lost consciousness and fell back to the *peepul* tree, dangling a few feet above the ground.

The ruler of Varanasi and his men had been watching the monkey king's incredible display of courage from below. The ruler ordered the monkey carefully cut down from the tree and placed on a velvet couch; he commanded his best physicians to tend his wounds.

When the monkey king regained consciousness the ruler asked him, "Why did you sacrifice yourself for the safety of the other monkeys?"

"I am their leader," said the monkey king. "I am like a father to them. It was up to me to do whatever I could to save them from the danger they faced."

"But in human kingdoms the multitude serves the king. The king does not serve them," said the ruler of Varanasi.

"Such may be the political ways of men," said the monkey, "but it is not the way of compassion. They all looked to me for help and I had to think of them rather than myself. Had I saved myself they would have all perished."

"But what have you gained yourself in disregarding your own welfare for the sake of others?" asked the ruler.

"I have gained the survival of my troop. I have also had the honor of serving as an example to you of how a true king rules with love and compassion over his subjects," and with those words the monkey king passed away.

The king of Varanasi sat with respect over the body of the monkey king. He ordered a royal cremation for the remains and then ordered his troops to all return to Varanasi taking not one fruit with them, leaving the tree to be the home of the great monkey king's troop.

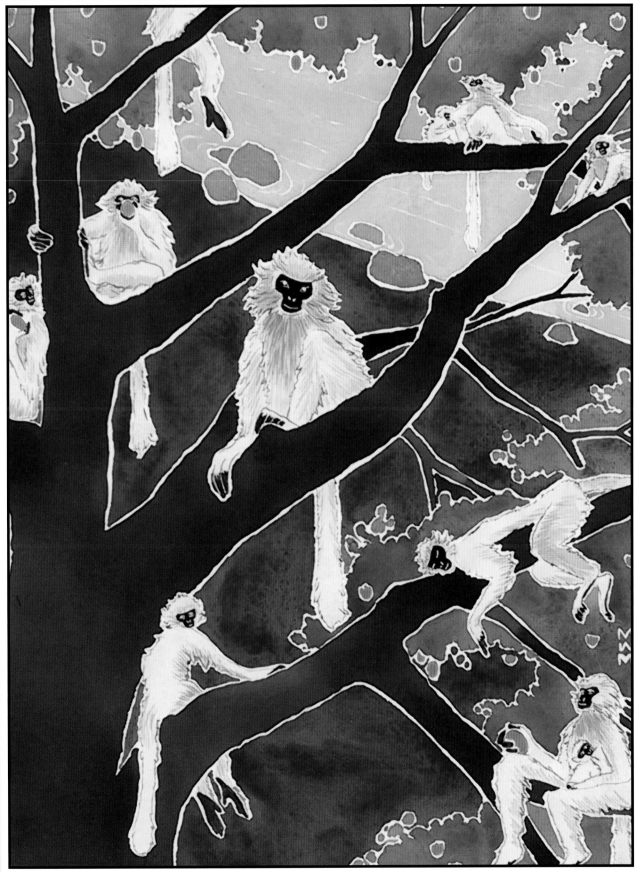

THE VULTURE

Long ago in northeast India near a place called Vulture's Peak there lived a wise vulture king who ruled a large flock. In doing their job of eating carrion, the vultures helped to keep their region clean and free of disease.

The king had a son who was very strong and large. The son was fortunate to have a wife who adored him and three fine children. With his keen eyesight and sharp sense of smell, which enabled him to detect carrion from a great distance, he was the envy of the flock. But he was admired most of all for his flying abilities. He could fly faster and higher than any other vulture, and he often did. In fact, he flew so high that his friends began to worry about him. They had heard that it was dangerous to fly to such heights and they told the king of their fear.

Concerned about his son's welfare, the king sent for his son. "I have heard," said the king, "that you have been flying very high into the sky. Is that true?" The son replied, "Yes, but it is not a danger for me. I am much stronger than my friends and have no difficulty in flying to great heights."

The king said, "We vultures are meant to fly only so high, and if we go beyond that point we will die. That applies to you as well as to all other vultures. When you are soaring high in the sky and the earth is but a small field in your vision, you have gone as far as you can, and you should go no further."

The son listened respectfully to his father and left, but the next time he was out flying with his friends he decided to impress them with his highest flight yet. He felt his strength and size made him different from other vultures and he wanted the others to observe his superiority. He caught a strong updraft from the mountains and started soaring higher and higher. Some of his friends were flying with him; they told him he was going too high, and they stopped their own ascent. He laughed at them and said he could go much higher. As he ascended he could see the earth become only a small field in his vision, as his father had said, but he kept on going. Upward he spiraled until he was completely out of sight from the ground. He felt invincible and went higher and higher. Then in a flash, as if he were struck by a blast of icy wind, he was unconscious. He lost all control of his flight and plummeted to the ground and was killed on impact.

The vulture's friends, father, wife, and children all gathered around his shattered body and wept.

THE WIND ANTELOPE

THE WIND ANTELOPE

Long ago in northeastern India in the great city of Varanasi a powerful king reigned from a palace of white marble inlaid with semiprecious stones. Surrounding his palace was a wonderful garden full of fruit trees, flowers, and rich, lush meadows.

One day the king's gardener noticed something very unusual in the garden: a wind antelope, considered to be the most timid of all wild creatures and rarely seen near human beings.

Every day the gardener brought fruit and flowers to the king from his garden. On this day the king casually asked the gardener if anything interesting had happened in the garden lately.

The gardener replied, "Why, yes your majesty. I was quite surprised to see a wind antelope in the garden this morning."

"That is indeed a surprise," said the king. "No one has ever captured such an antelope alive. Do you think you could capture the one you saw this morning?"

"Yes, your highness, I think that with a supply of honey I could eventually bring him right into the palace," said the gardener confidently.

This surprised and intrigued the king, and he told the gardener that he could have as much honey and other resources as he needed to achieve such a feat.

Early the next morning the gardener took a container of honey to the place he had seen the antelope grazing and smeared some honey on a section of the grass. He then concealed himself well and waited. After some time the timid antelope emerged from the forest that bordered the garden and began grazing. When he reached the honey-smeared grass he at first seemed surprised and backed off, but then he came forward again and licked the grass. Finding it to his liking, he eagerly ate all the grass that had honey on it. The antelope began to show up in the same area of the garden every morning to look for more honey-coated areas of grass. After some days the gardener slowly showed himself to the antelope from his hiding place. The antelope at first dashed into the woods, but the next day it returned, tempted by his memory of the sweet honey. This time when the gardener showed himself, the antelope did not run but stayed to finish his sweet grass. As the days passed the gardener moved closer and closer to the antelope until at last he was feeding the antelope honey-coated grass from his hand. At this point the gardener was sure that the antelope's craving for honey was an addiction. The antelope had lost his common sense and reasonable fear of humans due to his overpowering desire for the honey

The gardener then arranged for the path to the palace, the steps to the front door, and the entryway to be spread with a thick layer of grass. That morning the gardener was equipped with a large gourd of honey strapped to his shoulder and a bundle of grass tied to his waist. He began feeding the antelope the honey-coated grass in their regular place. But then he began walking backward on the grass covered path toward the palace, sprinkling a little of the sweetened grass in front of the antelope as he walked. The antelope kept his head down as he followed the trail, concentrating on not missing a morsel of the honey. They traveled down the path, up the steps, and directly into the palace. When they were inside the palace the servants slammed the door shut behind them. The startled antelope raised its head to find itself in a completely foreign environment, surrounded by polished marble and the king and his men stood staring at him. He panicked and tried to run in every direction, hoping to find a way out of the alien setting he had so foolishly walked into. He slipped on the polished floor and slid on his belly; in his terror he struggled back to his feet. The king watched the scene with pity.

He said, "The wind antelope is known to be so timid that it won't return for a week to a place that it has even glimpsed a human being, and it will not revisit a place where it has been startled for the rest of its life. But look at this poor creature: trapped by the craving and addiction it has, by his own doing, walked into a hell on earth for him."

The king instructed his men to open the palace doors and gently herd the antelope back outside. They did so, and the frightened creature dashed down the grass-covered stairs and into the woods, never to return to the palace or its gardens.

THE COMPASSIONATE APE

Long ago, in the foothills of the great Himalaya Mountains in northern India, a farmer worked a field with his pair of oxen. Late in the day he unyoked the oxen to graze while he cultivated by hand for a while; when he went to retrieve the beasts, they were nowhere to be found. Terribly upset at the loss of his precious oxen, he started to search for them, going deeper and deeper into the mountains.

Soon he was completely lost. Angry and hungry, he threw himself down under a tree. There he found several sour *tinduka* fruit. They tasted good to him, and he began searching for more. Not far away he found a great *tinduka* tree rooted in a rocky slope over the edge of a great waterfall that cascaded into a deep pit. The man climbed the tree, but while trying to pick ripe fruit he unwisely went too far, and the limb beneath him snapped cleanly off and both he and the branch plummeted down into the cavernous pit. Fortunately, he landed in the deep pool at the bottom, or he would have certainly been killed.

He managed to climb out of the pool and drag the branch of fruit along with him. Looking up he saw that the steep stone walls were impossible to climb, and he sat down and wept. Night fell, and he was beset by a swarm of mosquitoes that lived in the damp of the pit. For the next five days he survived on the few fruits that had fallen with him and water from the pool.

On the morning of the sixth day, a black ape visited the *tinduka* tree for its ripe fruit. He was a strong, beautiful ape with rich gray and black fur and a very gentle and compassionate nature. As he was climbing about the tree collecting fruit he heard a noise from the pit below. Looking down he saw the form of a gaunt man standing on the tallest rock in the pit and waving his hands.

The ape's heart went out to the man in such a sorry plight and he called down to him, "Good sir, what are you doing in such a place."

The man weakly responded, "Oh, kind ape, I lost my way looking for my oxen and fell into this horrible pit. I have no one to help me and I fear I will die of starvation soon."

The caring ape gathered up all the ripe fruit he could find, tossed it down to the man, and said, "Don't worry, I will think of some way to get you out of the pit." After long cogitation, the ape concluded that the only way to get the man out of the pit would be to carry him out on his back.

The ape climbed down the steep stone walls to the bottom of the pit. He greeted the man and said, "I have come to carry you out. You must climb on my back and hold on very tight."

The man bowed to the ape and said, "You are the most kind of animals. Thank you so much!"

With that the man clung to the ape's back. The man was a very heavy burden for the much smaller ape, and it was an extremely difficult and painful climb. At times the ape felt that his arms would be torn off from the great strain, but he persevered and finally reached the top of the pit. The man dismounted and the ape collapsed in utter exhaustion.

It was nearly dark and the ape desperately needed to rest. He said to the man, "There are many dangerous wild beasts in these woods. Please stand guard, and permit me to sleep for a while, and then I will do the same for you."

The man said, "I will keep a sharp eye out while you sleep. Sleep as long as you wish and get thoroughly refreshed."

While the ape slept the man began to fret. He thought, "With only fruit and roots to eat I will never be strong enough to find my way out of these mountains, but if I had the meat of this ape to eat, I would have plenty of strength to find my way home." He thought and thought while the ape slept, trying to rationalize his wicked plan.

Finally he built up sufficient evil courage to perform the deed. "After all," he said to himself, "he is just an ape, while I am a man. My life is worth more than his." And with that he took a large stone and threw it at the ape's head. But in his weakness he missed, and the stone only grazed the side of the animal's skull, bruising his temple.

The ape jumped to his feet to confront his attacker. After looking all about, he realized that it was the man he had just rescued who had attacked him. At first he was speechless in his amazement; then, great soul that he was, he was deeply saddened. Tears filled his eyes as he looked at the man. "How could you be capable of such an act?" he asked mournfully. "Instead of protecting me you try to slay me—and after I have just saved you from a sure and slow death. I may have taken you out of one abyss but you have, by your evil deed, just as surely plunged yourself into a pit of corruption even more fatal."

The man stood there trembling, sure that the powerful ape would crush him for his wickedness. Light was beginning to break over the mountains. To the man's amazement the ape said, "Come, I will take you to the edge of the mountain and show you the path to your village, but you walk in front of me, as you are not to be trusted in the least."

At the edge of the mountains the ape instructed the man how to reach his home. The man, overcome by the righteousness of the ape, was unable to speak. The ape's parting words were, "I have more compassion for you now than I did when you were at the bottom of that pit. Your evil deed will return on you multifold, for goodness returns goodness and wickedness returns wickedness."

THE COMPASSIONATE APE

The Jackal and the Rats

THE JACKAL AND THE RATS

L ong ago in the lush forest that surrounded Varanasi there lived a troop of rats. The leader of the rats was a noble creature, as kind and compassionate as he was large and strong. A wily jackal also lived in the forest. The jackal spent a great deal of time watching the rats, but he knew that their leader was too alert and cautious for him to catch any of the troop, so he decided to try a different strategy.

Knowing that the rat leader had the greatest respect for all things holy, the jackal decided to impersonate a holy being. He stationed himself on a path he knew the rats often took on their foraging expeditions, stood on one foot, opened his mouth slightly, and placed his front paws prayerfully together while facing the sun.

When the rat leader saw the jackal his first thought was to lead the troop in a different direction. But then he was intrigued by the strange appearance of the jackal. He went on ahead by himself and from a careful distance said, "Mr. Jackal, what is your name?

"Godly is what I am called," said the jackal.

"Why do you stand only on one leg?" queried the rat.

"If I were to stand on all four legs at once my weight would be too much for the poor earth to bear and I do not wish to hurt her," lied the jackal

"Why do you have you mouth open?" asked the rat.

"To take in air. I only eat the air, not wishing to harm any living thing," replied the deceitful jackal.

"And why do you hold your paws as such and face the sun?" inquired the rat.

"To praise and worship the sun, the giver of all life," said the false jackal.

The rat was very taken by the holiness of the jackal and thought to himself that this was a genuinely righteous creature from whom he and his troop could learn much. Beginning the next day he and the rest of the rats paid daily visits to the jackal to show their respect and listen to his teaching. But every day, as the troop left in its orderly single file, the jackal would quietly seize the last rat and quickly devour him, licking his lips before hastily assuming his holy stance again.

After a few days the leader noticed that the number of rats was diminishing, but he was at a loss as to why. He knew that the decline began only after they began visiting the jackal, and that the missing rats were always last seen on one of those visits. The leader concluded that somehow the jackal was behind the disappearances.

The next day, instead of walking at the head of his troop as the rats departed from the jackal, the rat leader took the last position. As he had guessed would happen, the jackal attacked him. But he was prepared and when the jackal charged, the rat leader lodged his teeth deep into his attacker's nose. The jackal let out a yelp that brought the entire troop of rats to the aid of their leader. They chased the jackal, biting at his flanks until he was far out of their territory. On the way home, the leader reflected, "What seems to be holy is sometimes profane."

The "weathermark" identifies this book as a production of Weatherhill, publishers of fine books on Asia and the Pacific. Editorial supervision: Jeffrey Hunter. Book and cover design: Liz Trovato. Production Supervision: Bill Rose. Printing and binding: OGP, China. The typefaces used are Weiss and Charlemagne.